S0-APY-991

THE STRANGE WONDERS OF ROOTS

EVAN GRIFFITH

Quill Tree Books
An Imprint of HarperCollins*Publishers*

Quill Tree Books is an imprint of HarperCollins Publishers.

 For information address HarperCollins Children's Books, a division of HarperCollins Publishers, 195 Broadway, New York, NY 10007.
www.harpercollinschildrens.com

Library of Congress Control Number: 2023944087
ISBN 978-0-06-328796-9
Typography by David Curtis
24 25 26 27 28 LBC 5 4 3 2 1
First Edition

For found families & chosen families

ONE

Holly sat at a bus stop beside a quiet road that twisted through green hills. A tree grew beside the bench. It was large and sprawling, with dark, cracked bark and tri-point leaves. Holly tugged her worn copy of the *Common Trees of the Eastern United States* guidebook out of her suitcase and confirmed her guess.

"Sugar maple," she announced to no one.

The tree rustled in the warm summer breeze. A leaf drifted down and landed in Holly's hair. She pocketed the leaf, then watched a small car crest the nearest hill and rumble to a stop in front of the bench.

Holly hadn't seen Uncle Vincent since three Christmases ago when he'd visited her and her dad for the holidays. Still, she recognized him as he stepped out of the car: scraggly eyebrows perched over winter-gray eyes, a salt-and-pepper beard, a nearly bald head. Definitely balder than three Christmases ago. A little less pepper and a little more salt in the beard, too.

It was strange, Holly thought, how Uncle Vincent looked exactly like her dad and not at all like him at the same time. It was like meeting her dad in a parallel universe—if middle-of-nowhere Vermont counted as a parallel universe.

"I hope you haven't been waiting long. I don't drive very often, and . . ." Uncle Vincent's voice was like the wind, always trailing away. Holly remembered this.

"It's fine," said Holly.

Uncle Vincent looked at her uncertainly. He seemed to be considering giving her a hug—extending his arms, then dropping them. Finally, he reached for her suitcase instead.

"I've got it," Holly said.

"Are you sure? It looks heavy."

"I've been carrying it all day." Holly heard the bite in her voice. Her words had been biting a lot lately. She wasn't sure what to do about it.

"Oh," said Uncle Vincent softly. "Of course." He opened the car's trunk. Holly tossed her fraying suitcase inside, then climbed into the passenger seat, still clutching *Common Trees of the Eastern United States.*

The car was old and cramped. The engine wheezed to

life when Uncle Vincent turned the key in the ignition. He patted the dashboard gently. "Music?" he asked.

"I don't care."

"Right. Me neither." Still, his hand hovered by the radio dial. After a few moments of silence, he turned it on. Classical music was playing but the signal was weak and staticky. "Arden isn't far. I would've picked you up from the airport, but . . ."

But he didn't drive very often. Holly nodded.

Uncle Vincent turned the car around and they slowly climbed the hill. The car groaned. Holly gripped the passenger door.

"So, everything went okay? The flights, and the bus?"

"Mm-hmm." This, Holly thought, was the key to not letting her words bite—saying very few words at all.

"I don't travel much myself. It makes me jittery, to tell you the truth."

Holly remembered going with her dad to pick up Uncle Vincent from the airport three Christmases ago. They had lived in Houston at the time, and the airport there was big and confusing. Uncle Vincent had gotten lost at baggage claim. When they'd finally found him, he was pale and shaky. Holly remembered her dad pulling to the side of the road on the way home so Uncle Vincent could throw up, and her dad laughing and saying, "Classic Vinny."

The memory made Holly feel a little nauseous herself.

Or maybe it was the winding country road. She pressed the book to her stomach.

"Did Alex—I mean, your dad—did he make it to San Francisco okay?" her uncle asked.

Holly checked her phone. There were a few texts from her mom—Did you land? Are you with your uncle? Did you pack enough socks?—but nothing from her dad. Yes, yes, and yes, she texted her mom. Then she made a time zone calculation in her head. "I don't think Dad has landed yet."

Her uncle glanced at her. "I hope he finds what he's looking for."

Early that morning at the Orlando airport, Holly's dad had told her, "This is it. My big break. I can *feel* it."

Then he'd caught his flight to San Francisco so he could perform in a small theater production of William Shakespeare's *A Midsummer Night's Dream.* He'd been cast as an understudy for one of the leads, which meant he'd only perform if the actor who actually got the role wound up getting sick. Until then, her dad was playing an extra: Woodland Sprite #4.

Holly, meanwhile, had caught a flight to New York City and a connection to Burlington, Vermont—a city she'd never heard of in a state she'd never been to, which was unusual. In the five years since her parents divorced, she'd lived in and visited a lot of places with her dad, who had a "thirst for adventure." That's what he called it, at least.

Holly called it "can't-make-up-his-mind syndrome," but only to herself.

"And your mom?" Uncle Vincent asked, fiddling with the radio dial as the static swelled. "Has her cruise started?"

Holly nodded. Usually, when her dad traveled without her, she went to stay with her mom, stepdad, and stepbrother in Virginia. But this summer, her stepdad, Ron, had surprised her mom and stepbrother with tickets for a Caribbean cruise vacation. So Holly's parents had decided that Holly should spend a month in Vermont with her uncle while her dad was chasing his big break and her mom was snorkeling, or sun-tanning, or whatever people did on cruises.

Holly tightened her grip on the passenger door. *I didn't want to go on a cruise, anyway,* she told herself. Again.

It was quiet in Uncle Vincent's car—just the hint of classical music fading in and out. Holly looked out the passenger window and tried to identify the trees they passed: Spruce. Ash. And . . . some kind of pine? She opened her book.

"Still a reader, I see," said Uncle Vincent.

Holly looked up and blinked. "What?"

"Last time I visited, you spent most of the week reading."

Holly shifted in her seat. "Well, I read nonfiction now. I'm twelve." She wasn't sure how, exactly, these two facts were related, but she felt there was some connection.

"You'll have to explore the shop. There are all kinds of old books—fiction, and nonfiction, and . . ."

Holly mentally reviewed the things she remembered about her uncle. He was younger than her dad by a year even though he'd always looked older. He was gay and lived alone in the tiny town of Arden, Vermont, where he owned some kind of bookstore. Holly's dad had gotten a kick out of the coincidence—"The forest in *A Midsummer Night's Dream* is called Arden, too," he'd said. "So we'll *both* be in Arden!" The bookstore had been another part of her dad's pitch for sending Holly to stay with her uncle: "You'll love hanging with Vinny. He's drowning in books."

Holly's brain began to buzz. What kinds of nonfiction did her uncle sell in his shop? Why were the books old? Where did they come from?

She swallowed the questions. Curiosity was a dangerous thing.

The road wound downhill and the radio signal grew stronger. As the music reached a crescendo, they passed a sign that read:

APPROACHING ARDEN

Then, in bigger letters:

HOME OF THE FAMOUS MADISON PLASTICS FACTORY!

They rounded a bend and Uncle Vincent smiled. It

wasn't her father's smile, big and flashy like the car salesmen on TV commercials. It was small and crooked and bright. "Arden," he said.

The town lay nestled in a valley between green hills like it was cupped in a giant's palm. Colorful homes clung to the slopes and clustered more densely in the valley, where they surrounded a factory with belching smokestacks. On one hill, perched over the town like an old, swollen sentinel, was a manor house.

But Holly's eyes were drawn to a wooded area near the center of town, right beside the factory in the heart of the giant's palm. The woods passed in and out of view as Uncle Vincent drove narrow streets past houses painted in faded blues and purples and greens.

At a stoplight, Holly looked down a side street. A boy on shiny roller skates was barreling down the street in hot pursuit of a small bouncy ball. As the light turned green, he spun out and crashed into a hedge. Holly considered alerting her uncle, but they were already driving away. And hedges weren't deadly, she reasoned. Still, she found herself thinking about the boy for a minute or two—worrying about him, even.

Then she noticed that several houses they passed had yard signs with an image of a tree and the words *Save the Grove.* She pointed at the wooded area in the center of town when it came into view again, and the question slipped out before she could swallow it: "Is that the grove?"

Uncle Vincent nodded. "Arden trees. That's what the town is named for. They only grow in this region."

"Why?" Holly blurted. "How?" Whenever she started asking questions it was hard to stop, like her unruly curiosity had broken out of its cage and she couldn't call it back.

"Something about the climate here, I believe. The trees are important to the town. And . . . some people are trying to cut them down. That's why we have to—"

"Save the grove," Holly said as Uncle Vincent parked the car in front of another yard sign. This one was defaced with spray paint: *Save our JOBS!*

"Oh dear," said Uncle Vincent. He hurried out of the car and tugged the sign out of the ground, then opened Holly's door for her. "Welcome home," he said, his eyes crinkling at the corners. "I mean, I know it's not *home.* But . . . I want you to make yourself at home while you're here."

Holly stepped out and looked up at a blue house that seemed to grow out of the hillside. Half of it sat precariously on stilts. A wooden staircase led from the street to the front door, past raised flowerbeds and garden gnomes. Trees grew behind and around the house—mostly gray and yellow birches.

Suddenly Holly felt an ache in the center of her chest. She wasn't sure if it was a good ache, because she thought the house was cute in a funny sort of way, or a bad ache, because Uncle Vincent was right. It wasn't home. Home was a place where things last, but nothing really lasts. This, according to Holly, was one of the three Fundamental Truths of Life.

One: Adults don't actually know that much more than kids (and sometimes they know less).

Two: Olive oil is good but olives are gross.

Three: Nothing lasts.

Except for trees, Holly thought as she looked at the birches. With the right conditions—and assuming they weren't burned or bothered—trees could live for a long, long time. Hundreds or even thousands of years. Their roots spread wide and burrowed deep, anchoring them, nourishing them, connecting them to each other and to the earth.

Holly looked down at her feet. Her tennis shoes were stained and scuffed. Then she took a deep breath and followed Uncle Vincent up the steps to the house that grew out of the hill.

TWO

The house wasn't small, exactly, but it was cramped. The rooms were boxy and full—a dining room barely big enough for its table, a kitchen overflowing with chipped chinaware and antique appliances. Mismatched chairs flanked a sunken couch in the living room and the fireplace mantel was lined with old photographs. Nature paintings hung on the walls, and everywhere—*everywhere*—there were books. Books in stacks, books on shelves, books filling a nook beneath a narrow staircase. Books with leather covers and yellowed pages. Books that looked like they might crumble to dust if they were disturbed.

"When I run out of room at the shop, I keep books here," said Uncle Vincent. It sounded like an apology. He set the defaced yard sign by the front door, then pushed a stack of books closer to the wall, widening the path for Holly down the hall. She picked up the top book from the stack. *Notes from the London Zoological Society Conference on Animal Ecology.*

"I'm not sure if you remember—and it's okay if you don't!—but I'm an antiquarian. The books I collect and sell . . . they're pretty old."

Holly opened the book to the title page and saw the publication year: 1927. The book felt precious now, and Holly held it lightly as she turned the funny word over in her head. *Antiquarian.* So many syllables. She set the book back on top of the stack.

"Help yourself to anything in the pantry," Uncle Vincent said as she followed him down the hall, wheeling her squeaky suitcase behind her. "I'm not much of a cook, but . . . The TV has cable. I don't have those streaming services, but if there are any shows you want . . ." Every sentence ran away from him. Holly wondered where they all went.

He paused at the foot of the stairs. "Your room is up here." Then, looking at her suitcase: "May I?"

No, Holly nearly said. It was what she'd said to the man on the airplane who offered to carry her suitcase down the aisle for her. It was what she'd said to the bus driver who asked if Holly needed a hand when she was boarding. But now her arms were tired, and the steps were narrow and uneven, and she only shrugged. Uncle Vincent picked up her suitcase and she followed him up, feeling grateful and grumpy at the same time.

The creaky stairs ended in a tiny room with a sloped ceiling that nearly grazed Holly's head and forced Uncle Vincent to duck. A skinny bed was squeezed inside, along with a small wardrobe and a desk, both made of worn, dark wood.

But there were windows—one on each wall, looking out over the trees that surrounded the house and flooding the room with dappled light. Squirrels scampered along the branches of the trees, chattering brightly, while birds that Holly couldn't see sang songs she'd never heard before.

"I know it's small," Uncle Vincent said, "but I hope it's okay. The whole house is yours. The yard, too. And the town! This—it's just a place to sleep."

Holly turned and saw a vase of flowers on the desk. Every bloom stretched toward the nearest window. She didn't know what the flowers were—she didn't know flowers like she knew trees—but even with her stuffed-up nose, Holly could smell them. Fresh-cut, she guessed. The word unfurled in her mind: *beautiful.*

"It's fine," she said.

"Oh—I emptied the wardrobe so you can unpack. And if you need any help . . ." Holly shook her head. Uncle Vincent nodded. "Are you hungry? I think I can throw together some grilled cheeses without burning the house down." He chuckled nervously.

Holly knew she should be hungry—she'd barely eaten all day—but her stomach was still unsettled and she felt a sudden and urgent desire to be alone. "I'm going to rest for a bit."

She wasn't sure if her uncle was relieved or disappointed. His face didn't move like her dad's. It had different creases. "Of course. If you change your mind . . ."

Holly listened to his footsteps receding down the creaky stairs, then lay on top of the bed. It was softer than she'd expected.

For a while she stared at the sloping ceiling. She was tired—from two plane rides, and the airport shuttle, and the bus, and the drive—but she knew she wouldn't fall asleep. And not just because she was in a strange room in a strange house, and not just because the house shook on its stilts when the wind blew. Holly just wasn't any good at napping. She chased naps but they eluded her. On the verge of sleep, she always met her racing heart.

Holly checked her phone. There was a text from her dad: Landed!

She pictured it all in her head: her dad barreling off the plane and dashing through the airport, hungry for the sights and sounds of a new city. He would hail a cab, flash his megawatt smile, then ask the driver to take the long way round to the apartment he was renting. He'd rack up the world's largest taxi fare while entertaining the driver with witty banter and checking all the dating apps on his phone. Whenever he went somewhere new, Holly's dad found lots of local women to meet for dinner and drinks.

She had another text, too. Hi, Holly! How's your summer going? This was from Abigail, a girl who had sat next to Holly in Ms. Wilkins's sixth-grade science class. They had chatted a few times and they'd exchanged numbers so they could coordinate when they were both chosen to bring desserts to their class's end-of-year party. Holly stared at the message for a minute, surprised and flustered, then tossed her phone aside without responding.

Thanks to her dad's "thirst for adventure," she hadn't stayed in one town or one school for more than a year since her parents divorced. She'd spent her sixth-grade year in Winter Park, Florida, just outside Orlando—but by the time the new school year rolled around, she figured she'd be somewhere new again.

So there wasn't much point in responding to Abigail. Holly had promised herself a long time ago that she wouldn't make friends she'd just have to leave. It was the only rational approach, she thought. After all, the third Fundamental Truth of Life applied to friendships, too. Nothing lasts.

She busied herself with *Common Trees of the Eastern*

United States. She was just checking the index to see if there was anything about arden trees when a yelping sound outside drew her to the window that faced the street. There, sprawled on the sidewalk by Uncle Vincent's house, was the boy in the shiny roller skates. He had tripped over a fallen branch, it seemed, and now his bouncy ball was bouncing down the street without him.

Holly huffed. What was this boy doing, roller-skating around town without knowing *how* to roller-skate? And was he okay? And did Holly need to *do* something?

Thankfully, Uncle Vincent hurried outside and helped the boy stand. Inexplicably, the boy was grinning from ear to ear. Holly cracked open the window so she could hear what he was saying.

"Sorry about your sign, Mr. V. I saw it earlier. I'm gonna catch whoever did that and teach them a lesson." The boy waved a knuckled fist in the air.

Uncle Vincent laughed. "Don't worry about that, Lionel. Are you okay? Are you bleeding? I have bandages inside . . ."

"I'm good! That was a fun fall. And it only hurts a medium amount."

Holly squinted at the boy. He looked about her age, maybe a little younger. He wore elbow pads and kneepads and tall, striped socks. His pale skin was sunburned and his hair was disheveled, perhaps on account of crashing into the bushes. She thought she spied a leaf in his hair, which reminded her of the maple leaf in her pocket.

"Is your niece here yet?" the boy said. "Today's the day!"

Holly gulped. Were people . . . *expecting* her?

"She just arrived," said Uncle Vincent. "But she's resting now."

"Aw, man," said the boy. "I was gonna say hi! Is she staying up there?" Suddenly the boy was pointing directly at Holly's window—directly at *her*. She scrambled away from the glass, hoping she hadn't been spotted.

For a minute, she heard the muffled voices of Uncle Vincent and the boy, Lionel. Then it was quiet again. She peeked out the window. The boy was skating down the street and around a bend, probably on his way to crash into something else.

Holly sat cross-legged on the bed. Her heart was still racing. She thought about unpacking her suitcase, then shook her head. This wasn't her room. This wasn't her house. She would only be here for a month. Maybe less, if her dad gave up on the play before then. It wouldn't be the first time he quit halfway through a gig. So she'd live out of her suitcase, she decided, until it was time to go back to Florida, or wherever her dad dragged her next.

Still, she took the maple leaf out of her pocket and set it on the desk next to the flowers.

THREE

For the rest of the afternoon, Holly curled up on the bed, rereading *Common Trees of the Eastern United States* and almost-but-not-quite napping. She thought about getting under the covers, but it felt too soon to unmake the bed—too soon to disturb a room she didn't know.

Uncle Vincent checked on her a couple times. Once, he brought her a steaming mug of herbal tea. "Ginger turmeric," he said. Holly had never had hot tea before and she didn't know what turmeric was. She sniffed the brew, crinkled her nose, and left it on top of the wardrobe, peeking at it every few minutes over the top of her book.

The book was full of sticky notes and scribbled annotations from when Holly had researched tree root systems for her sixth-grade science report, "The Strange Wonders of Roots." Ms. Wilkins had told the class that a good report name makes someone want to read it right away. She said Holly's title was strong because the words *strange* and *wonders* are enticing.

But Ms. Wilkins was also the one who said, months later, that the project was over and Holly should stop reading books about trees when she was supposed to be paying attention to a genetics lesson, or drawing a human cell, or labeling all the bones on Skelly, the class skeleton.

Holly never figured out how to tell Ms. Wilkins that, ever since her report, her mind had been stuck on trees. That sometimes she saw oaks and cypresses and weeping willows behind her eyelids. That her dreams were full of trees—tall, spindly trees and short, stubby trees; trees she could climb and trees with hollows where she could hide.

Now Holly stared at the book's entry on dwarf palmettos, which were common in Florida. Her eyes traced the text but her mind recited the sealed note that her latest guidance counselor had asked her to deliver to her dad one day. *Holly shows a strong aptitude for science, especially environmental science, but she's struggling to find her social footing. I hear from her teachers that she rarely engages with her classmates, even when they try to include her. I suggest Holly join a sports team or an after-school club. Perhaps the Recorder Ensemble? Her music teacher says she has potential!* Holly had thrown the note away.

Uncle Vincent's house trembled in the wind and a chill passed through the room, bringing Holly back to the present. She sat up, rubbed her arms, and watched the sky turn orangey-purple through the windows. Her stomach groaned. She tried to ignore it. Her little room felt strange, but the idea of leaving it felt even stranger. But the growl was insistent. Holly sighed. The human body was so exasperating.

She ventured downstairs and found Uncle Vincent sitting on the couch in front of a tray table covered in paper and paints and brushes. On the TV, a funny-looking man with puffy hair was painting a snowy mountain on a canvas.

Uncle Vincent stood up so fast he nearly kicked over his tray table, then hit Pause on a DVD player. Holly was surprised to find that DVD players still existed. "Did you get some sleep?" he asked.

"Yes," Holly lied.

"Good. You must be hungry now! I have frozen dinners. I wasn't sure what you like, so I picked up lots of options. There's ravioli, and pad Thai, and . . ."

Holly peeked at his painting in progress. It was a close match to the painting on the TV, but a little softer and more pastel. Tiny streaks of green suggested a tree line—probably conifers, Holly thought, like pine and spruce.

She followed him into the kitchen and chose an enchilada

dinner from a crowded freezer. Uncle Vincent went with a calzone.

While Holly's food was in the microwave, her eyes roamed the cramped kitchen. Antique pans and dishes filled every nook and cranny. Holly wondered why a man who didn't cook had so much cookware.

They ate at the dining table. An uncertain silence stretched between them. Holly was used to her dad filling silences. He always had an anecdote to share or a joke to tell. But Uncle Vincent seemed as unsure of what to say as she did. He even ate differently than her dad—quieter, with less clattering of silverware and not a single burp.

Holly shivered. She was used to visiting different places, but there was always a moment in a new environment—after the flurry of travel and arrival—when the strangeness of being somewhere unfamiliar swept over her. She was *here.* But what did *here* mean?

She was glad when Uncle Vincent broke the silence. "How do you like Winter Park?" He frowned after asking it, like he wasn't quite sure it was the right place to start.

Holly shrugged. "It's fine. Kind of boring."

"It must be a big change from DC and Boston. Is it more like Houston?"

Holly was surprised that Uncle Vincent could so easily name the last three places she'd lived with her dad. She hadn't spoken to her uncle in years. How much did her dad speak to him, she wondered—and how much did her uncle know about *her*?

"I guess," she said, spinning her fork through globs of cheesy enchilada sauce. "They're both hot. And they have some trees in common." She blushed and shoved a forkful of enchilada into her mouth. Ever since she'd been scolded by Ms. Wilkins for spending too much time thinking about trees, she'd tried not to talk about them so much.

"I saw that you were reading about trees earlier," Uncle Vincent said, looking at her with interest. Holly thought of telling him about her science report, but she took another bite of enchilada instead.

Her uncle tried again: "Do you have friends in Winter Park?"

Holly thought of the text from Abigail. "Not really."

Uncle Vincent's brow crinkled. "It must be challenging, moving around so much."

Holly looked at him sharply. "I get to see lots of things. A lot more than most kids."

"Oh, of course." He opened his mouth again, then shut it. A moment later, he smiled. "Your dad sent me pictures from your trip to New York City back in March. That must've been fun!"

Holly thought back to the trip. She remembered racing around the city with her dad, gawking at skyscrapers and laughing together when they found someone blowing giant bubbles through the world's biggest bubble wand in Central Park. She remembered, too, reading alone in their hotel room while her dad auditioned for local plays and went on dates.

"It was okay," she said quietly.

Uncle Vincent's smile wavered. "Your dad seems excited about this role he's landed in San Francisco. He said it might lead to some bigger opportunities."

"Maybe," said Holly. Then, because she couldn't help herself: "Woodland Sprite Number Four. That's his role. I mean, he's an understudy for Lysander, one of the main characters. But he'll only get to play Lysander if the other guy playing Lysander catches a cold or something."

She thought back to her dad's words at the Orlando airport. *This is it. My big break.* But was it? He'd said that so many times before, each time like it was the first. Holly was reminded of the first Fundamental Truth of Life: Adults don't actually know that much more than kids (and sometimes they know less).

"He's always enjoyed performing," said Uncle Vincent. "Even back in high school. Drama club and all that. He used to ask me to practice lines with him, then got mad at me for mumbling . . ."

Holly wasn't sure how to respond. It felt odd to learn something new about her dad, who she knew well, from her uncle, who she hardly knew at all.

As another silence fell between them, Holly's eyes roamed. She looked at the painted canvases on the walls—beaches, pastures, waterfalls—and the collection of wooden figurines in the center of the dining table. Some were animals; others were abstract.

"I take classes at the arts center here in town," Uncle Vincent said. "They teach drawing, painting, ceramics, woodworking—"

"Is that based on the grove?" Holly asked, pointing to a painting of trees. The perspective was like looking up at the treetops. Hazy light filtered down through the branches and the trees seemed to shimmer.

Uncle Vincent nodded. "I've always loved the grove. I think you'll like it, too—especially if you're interested in trees." He reached into his pocket and pulled out a small, round pin. He handed it to Holly. It had a simple graphic of a tree, the same graphic that was on the yard signs around town. "I made the logo for the Save the Grove Committee. I'm one of the committee's founding members, and I host our meetings every other Monday. Our next meeting is tomorrow night, actually. You're welcome to join us! There's always good food . . ."

Holly felt it again: curiosity, lifting its head and sniffing the air like a bear on the first warm day of spring. She turned the pin between her fingers. "Who wants to cut down the grove?"

"Did you see the big factory when we drove into town?"

Holly nodded.

"That's the Madison Plastics Factory. The owners, Mr. and Ms. Madison, want to clear the grove and expand the factory grounds with a visitors' center and a museum about the history of the factory."

Holly crinkled her nose. "The history of a plastics factory? That's boring. Who'd want to go to that?"

"Well, the factory is a big part of Arden's history. It employs about half the folks in town."

"So half the folks in town could've spray-painted your sign."

Uncle Vincent's brow furrowed. "I suppose so. It's . . . a delicate issue."

More questions stirred in Holly's mind. Why did the Madisons have to build the factory expansion *there*? How would a visitors' center and a museum save the town's jobs? If these arden trees were so rare, shouldn't they be preserved? And who went around cutting down beautiful trees, anyway? But this time she managed to wrangle her curiosity back into its cage. She set the pin down on the table and slid it over to her uncle.

More cheerfully, he said, "I was thinking after dinner we could take a stroll downtown, and I could show you a few things. I also picked up a board game the other day, if you'd like to try it. I don't know if you like board games, or . . ."

"I'm still pretty tired."

Uncle Vincent dropped his gaze to the table. "Travel days are exhausting. But maybe tomorrow you can explore town? I have to work at the shop, but you can come and go as you like." He got up and disappeared down the hall, then returned with a key. "I had a copy made for you."

He dropped the key into her palm. It felt strangely heavy.

"Oh—and your mom mailed me some kind of toothpaste for you . . . ?"

Holly's cheeks burned. She didn't like people to know that a dentist had prescribed her a special toothpaste for highly sensitive gums. She didn't like *being* someone with highly sensitive gums. But her mom never let her forget it. It was annoying, especially because Holly had already brought plenty of the toothpaste with her. But it was also nice. If her mom was still thinking about her teeth, her mom was still thinking about *her*, even when she was busy having the best time ever in the Caribbean with her new family. "Thanks," Holly mumbled.

She tried to clean the table—she often cleaned up after dinners with her dad—but Uncle Vincent insisted that she take it easy, so she excused herself.

Before she went upstairs, she paused in front of the fireplace and inspected the framed photographs on the mantel. Several were old family portraits—Holly's dad and Uncle Vincent as kids, with much younger-looking versions of Holly's grandparents, who had both died when Holly was little. She wondered why she'd never seen any of the pictures before.

After she brushed her teeth with her prescription toothpaste, she lay awake in bed for a while, heart pounding. The first night in a new place was always hard. The strangeness of it all was even stranger in the dark. But slowly the whispering birches lulled her into a fitful sleep.

It was late morning when Holly woke. She was warm. The sun streamed through the windows of her room, casting tree shadows on the wall like her own personal mural.

She knew at once that Uncle Vincent wasn't home—not just because he'd already told her he was working today, but because she knew the feeling of an empty house. It was a specific silence, the certainty that you could speak and nobody would hear you. Even when he wasn't traveling, her dad never spent much time at home. There were always new restaurants to try, new shows to see, new people to meet.

She checked her phone for the time and found messages from both her parents waiting for her. From her mom, a photo of her five-year-old stepbrother, Topher, cannonballing into a pool on the cruise-ship deck. He was wearing bright orange swim trunks and smiling a gap-toothed smile. Miss you, hon! her mom had texted.

Her dad had sent a picture, too: a selfie of him on a pier with a bunch of seals suntanning around him. San Francisco is HEAVEN. You would love it. How's it going with Vinny?

Holly had never been to San Francisco, but she doubted it was heaven. For her dad, any new place was heaven until it wasn't anymore. Sometimes Holly wondered what that was like—finding heaven everywhere you went, then losing it, over and over again.

Fun, she texted Mom. Fine, she texted Dad.

She tugged fresh clothes out of her suitcase, changed, and went downstairs. On her way to the kitchen, she ran her finger along the spines of old books on shelves. She expected her finger to come away dusty, but it was clean.

She rummaged through the overstuffed kitchen cabinets for coffee grounds but only found tea. Anxiety stirred. She usually started each day with a cup of black coffee, even though her newest pediatrician said kids shouldn't have so much caffeine.

With a frown, she chose the most caffeinated tea option—Irish Breakfast—and microwaved a mug of water. When it was piping hot, she dunked the bag and swirled it around, feeling the house contract and expand around her like old wooden lungs.

While the tea steeped, she noticed the handwritten note on the counter. Parts of it were crossed out and scribbled over like it had been revised several times.

> Off to work. ~~If you aren't too tired~~ If you feel up to it, would you mind popping by Annie's Market and picking up a box of maple scones for tonight's Save the Grove meeting? ~~Annie is a good friend of~~ The market is at the corner of Cornelia Street and Opal Lane. I thought you might have fun finding it with a real map!
>
> —Vincent
>
> PS ~~I'd be delighted if you also visited~~ Feel free to stop by the bookshop, too.

Beneath the note was a twenty-dollar bill and a creased map of Arden. While she drank her tea and ate a not-quite-ripe banana she found in a fruit basket, she traced the roads on the map until her finger landed on the intersection of Cornelia Street and Opal Lane. It was downtown, by the factory and a splotch of green on the map. The grove.

She stared at the map for a long time. She had the funny feeling the house was holding its breath.

"Maybe later," she said.

The house sighed.

She returned to her room to read. In addition to *Common Trees of the Eastern United States,* she'd packed a couple other books about nature that she'd bought at a school book fair. But her heart was racing again and she couldn't focus. After a few pages, she threw her book down and marched downstairs.

"Fine. Now."

She grabbed the twenty-dollar bill from the counter, leaving the map behind. Who used an actual map, Holly wondered, when a smartphone could get you anywhere?

But there *was* something charming about the map. The oldness of the paper. The creases suggesting its use. It reminded Holly of the books that filled Uncle Vincent's home—old, and precious for its oldness. So, on second thought, she pocketed the map, too. Then she stepped outside, locking the door behind her with the key Uncle Vincent had given her.

The town of Arden lay spread before her, bright and sparkling in the morning light. She rolled her shoulders back, then began the downhill walk toward the heart of town.

FOUR

It was a short walk downtown from Uncle Vincent's, but Holly took her time, pausing to stare at the houses that lined the gently sloping street.

Holly's most recent home, a townhouse she shared with her dad in Florida, was identical to the townhouses next to it—identical, in fact, to every townhouse on their street. White paint, pink shutters, a single foxtail palm growing in the same spot in each tiny front yard. Even the mailboxes were uniform: lime green, a color Holly guessed was meant to be cheerful but was actually a little sickening.

But each house in Arden was unique. Colorful bungalows sprouted from the ground like strange beasts, gazing inquisitively back at Holly with windows for eyes. Some were squat. Some were tall and skinny. Some were small but others were large and patchwork, like each part of the house had been built at a different time and none of the parts quite matched.

At first, the street seemed deserted. But then Holly noticed the animals—a fat cat lounging on a warm car roof; a pair of squirrels bickering up in the trees; a row of birds perched on a telephone line, staring down at Holly with beady eyes.

Then there was the tortoise.

It was a very large tortoise, walking up the street ever-so-slowly toward Holly. Behind the tortoise shuffled an elderly woman. They both froze a few yards away from Holly. The tortoise seemed to smile but the woman scowled. She was impossibly old, with pale, papery skin, an ill-fitting auburn wig, and giant glasses that made her eyes buggy.

"Don't crowd Henry," the woman croaked. "He's claustrophobic."

"I'm not—" Holly began, but the woman's face was a sour pickle, and Holly swallowed the rest of her protest. She stepped aside so the woman and the tortoise could pass. It took a while.

For a minute, Holly watched them continue on up the street. *Is the tortoise her pet? Did it actually just smile at me? Can tortoises really be claustrophobic?* She shook away the questions and reminded herself of her mission: maple scones.

When the road forked, she consulted Uncle Vincent's town map. A right turn on Cornelia Street brought her downtown, which sat at the lowest point of the valley. Here, instead of houses, there were businesses: Wilson's Records 'n' More, with a window display of turntables and vinyl albums. The Madison Arts Center, with signs advertising classes in painting, pottery, and woodworking. Miss Maisie's Wig Emporium, sitting on the corner of a little town square.

Holly cupped her eyes and peered through the window of Miss Maisie's, wondering if this was where the tortoise walker had purchased her auburn wig. But when the spindly, pink-haired shopkeeper popped her head out and said, "Are you ready for a *shocking* transformation?" Holly hurried away without a word.

She tried not to make eye contact with anyone she passed on the street—not the lady with the tote bag full of baguettes, or the old couple handing out religious pamphlets, or the man with the bowler hat leaning against a streetlamp, tossing and catching a copper penny. But they all seemed intent on making eye contact with *her.* They looked at her curiously—kindly, even—but Holly averted her eyes.

She found Annie's Market at the corner of Cornelia and Opal. Beneath a cherry-red awning there was a sign taped to the glass: *Now Hiring! Inquire Inside.* Holly slipped into the market, glad to escape the town's gaze. But she immediately drew the attention of the woman in a yellow dress and floral apron standing behind the register.

"Hi there!" the woman said. "Are you here to inquire about the opening? I saw you looking at the sign. You might be a little too young, dear, but—" She clasped her hands together. "Oh, I'm so silly. Holly Foster. It *is* you, isn't it?"

Holly's stomach lurched. Here was hard evidence: people in Arden *were* expecting her. "How did you—"

"Vincent said you'd be coming to stay with him. My goodness, you two look just alike!"

"Um," said Holly, wondering how, exactly, she looked like a forty-five-year-old bearded and balding man. She took a closer look at the woman's face—twinkling eyes and round, rose-tinted cheeks; a smile so bright it felt like a punch—then at her name tag: Annie.

"I'm looking for maple scones," said Holly.

"The traditional snack of the Save the Grove meetings! I told Vincent I'd bring some tonight. I always do. But you're welcome to take them now." Annie fetched a box of scones from a table near the register.

"You're coming to the meeting at Uncle Vincent's?" Holly asked.

Annie pointed to the Save the Grove pin on her lapel.

"A proud founding member of the committee. We're so excited for you to join us!"

"I'm not—I'm just here for the scones."

"Oh . . . Well, that's okay, too!" Annie handed Holly the box of scones. When Holly set her uncle's twenty-dollar bill on the counter by the register, Annie waved it away. "Did Vincent really think I'd let you pay? This store might not be here much longer, but as long as it is, the Save the Grove Committee gets complimentary scones!"

Annie smiled again, and—without meaning to—Holly smiled back. It annoyed Holly, the way smiles were contagious. It annoyed her, too, how Annie had already made her want to ask questions. *Why might the market not be here much longer?*

Then Holly saw a stack of CDs by the register—*Blue Jazz Expressions* by Reggie Summers—and she only had more questions. *What's blue jazz? And who still buys CDs?* But she had the feeling she often got when talking to a stranger: a timer had run out. It was time to go.

As she turned to leave, the shop door opened. A man and two teenagers—a girl and a boy—walked in. Annie's smile tightened. "Hi, Mr. Madison," she said. "Hi, Elise and Ray."

Holly froze. When Uncle Vincent had told her about Mr. Madison, the factory owner, she'd imagined a large man with a handlebar mustache and maybe a top hat, too. But the real Mr. Madison was a man of average height, dressed in a drab sweater and slacks. His hairline was receding and his facial features were small, like they were sinking into his sandy skin. He looked around the market with an air of discomfort, giving Holly a cursory glance before his gaze landed on Annie's Save the Grove pin.

"Can I help you find anything today?" Annie asked.

"It's bring-your-kids-to-work day at the factory," Mr. Madison said. His voice was quiet—not soft-quiet like Uncle Vincent's, but shaky-quiet, like he wasn't getting enough air. "Ray forgot his lunch."

"I said sorry," the teenage boy drawled without looking up from his phone.

The teenage girl—Elise, Holly deduced—crossed her arms. "I *didn't* forget my lunch, but I want something else."

Mr. Madison smiled thinly. "A good excuse to support another local business." He tugged a wallet out of his pocket and dropped a credit card on the counter. The card was very shiny. "Grab what you'd like, kids. Quickly—my next meeting starts in twenty."

Holly lingered on the threshold of the shop as Ray and Elise rummaged through a refrigerator of premade sandwiches and salads. There was something about Mr. Madison and his kids that felt a little familiar, but she wasn't sure what. She was sure she'd never seen them before.

Then she thought about the vandalized sign in Uncle

Vincent's yard—*Save Our JOBS!*—and she felt a flush of anger. This was the family who wanted to tear down the grove so they could expand their factory.

Ever since she'd researched trees for her science report, the idea of deforestation—removing trees to make room for something else—had irked Holly. She knew that trees were incredibly complex living beings. She knew, too, that science was only beginning to unearth all their secrets. Plus, the world *needed* trees, and it had already lost so many. Couldn't the Madisons find another plot of land? Couldn't they leave the arden trees alone? She clenched her fists, took a step forward . . .

. . . then shook her head. *None of my business*, she told herself. *I'll be out of here in a month—maybe less, if Dad gets sick of being Woodland Sprite #4.*

"Who are you?"

Elise was staring at her with heavy-lidded eyes. She had asked the question in a bored sort of way, like the answer didn't actually matter.

"Oh, that's—" Annie began.

"No one," said Holly. "I mean . . . I was just leaving." She slipped out of the market before Elise could ask more questions. In a new town, it was best to remain a stranger, she reckoned. A stranger was left alone. A stranger wasn't tied down. A stranger could leave at any moment without consequence.

But Annie already knew her name. *Holly Foster! It* is *you, isn't it?* And then there was the boy with the roller skates. *Is your niece here yet? Today's the day!* Holly had the squirmy suspicion that it was already too late to be a stranger in Arden.

She collected herself on the sidewalk, inhaling the downtown air—factory smoke blended with an earthier, woodsy scent. She looked up and down the street. If she turned right, she could start the walk back to Uncle Vincent's. But if she turned left . . .

The fate of the grove really *wasn't* her business, and she was *sure* she'd be gone long before it was resolved, but there wasn't any harm in taking a peek at the arden trees, was there? Especially if it was just for her own tree research?

She walked farther down Cornelia Street. She soon passed the Arden Antiquarian Shop. *Books, Records, Ephemera!* a sign proclaimed. The shop was a stone's throw from Annie's Market. If Uncle Vincent worked so close to Annie's, Holly thought, why couldn't he pick up the maple scones? Or why not let Annie bring them to the meeting?

She approached the shop window. Old books lined a table facing the window, along with another stack of *Blue Jazz Expressions* CDs. "This town must really like Reggie Summers," Holly murmured.

Beyond the window display were several rows of wooden shelves overflowing with books. And there, sitting behind a desk at the back of the shop, was her uncle. He was holding a magnifying glass to a scrap of paper and studying it by lamplight. His whole body curled around the scrap, like—for right now, at least—that scrap was his entire world.

Holly thought about going inside, but when Uncle Vincent looked up, Holly ducked beneath the window. She wasn't sure why, only that she was embarrassed. She power walked away from the shop and didn't slow down until she reached the factory a few minutes later.

It was a brick behemoth of a building surrounded by a gated iron fence. Smokestacks reached like ashen fingers for the sky, spewing charcoal-gray smoke over downtown. The name MADISON was spelled out in giant letters across the building's facade. Holly thought about Mr. Madison, with his drab sweater and shaky voice. He wasn't nearly as imposing as his factory.

Cornelia Street ended just past the factory at a dense line of trees—the edge of the grove. The woodsy scent was stronger here and the world was quieter.

Holly surveyed the arden trees. They were tall and thin, but they blossomed at the crown. Slender branches stretched up and out, knitting together and forming a broad canopy. The trees' bark was an unusual silvery color that shimmered in the morning light just like in Uncle Vincent's painting of the grove.

Holly's pulse drummed in her ears. Sometimes curiosity was like hunger. Sometimes it burned. She wanted—she *needed*—to study the trees more closely. So she took one step forward, then another, until the grove enveloped her.

FIVE

In the grove, everything was a whisper—the crunch of leaves underfoot, the rustling of branches in the wind, the burbling of a small creek that wound through the trees. There were birds, but they chirped softly, as if they were sharing secrets. Even the squirrels scampered lightly here.

Holly stepped lightly, too, feeling like she'd entered a sacred space. Not a cold sort of sacred place, like the church she went to with her mom and Ron and Topher when she visited them in Virginia. No, the grove felt like a warm sacred place, where breathing is easier and the world comes into focus.

It was how Holly often felt when she was surrounded by trees, from the pine brush of Florida to the hill country cedars of Texas and the northern hardwood forests of

Massachusetts. It was why she'd studied trees for her science report. She liked the solidity of trees. She liked that they didn't move, even if you closed your eyes or turned away. She liked that they didn't ask you to speak, or smile, or do anything you didn't feel like doing. Most of all, she liked the way her mind felt in a forest, the way her mind felt right now: quiet but sharp.

A gust of wind parted the canopy overhead. As dappled sunlight fell into the grove and illuminated the arden trees' silvery bark, Holly pictured *Common Trees of the Eastern United States* and mentally turned the pages, looking for connections and points of comparison. The pale, slender trunks reminded her of birches and aspens, but the broad, pronged leaves—as big as Holly's palm—were more like a maple's.

She placed a hand against the nearest trunk and was surprised by the bark. It looked smooth, but it was textured, with tiny ridges forming intricate patterns. "What are you?" she whispered, then scolded herself. Scientists didn't talk to trees. They investigated them methodically. So she continued her investigation.

Parts of the grove were carpeted in thick bushes and tall grass, but there were patches of bare ground, too, where roots were visible beneath fallen leaves. Holly fell to her knees and traced the snaking roots. At times, it was hard to tell which roots belonged to which tree; each tendril vanished belowground, then reappeared elsewhere, intertwining with other roots and branching in countless directions.

Holly set down the box of maple scones so she could crawl along the path of a single root; losing it here, picking it up again there as it curled around a cluster of blueish-white mushrooms. Her heart raced—not in the can't-sleep sort of way, but in the verge-of-a-discovery sort of way. The arden trees had one of the most complicated root systems she'd ever seen, and the mushrooms made her wonder . . .

She tugged a loose root tendril out of the earth and brushed away soil. The root's tips were covered in a network of fine white lace. A fungus, Holly guessed. She'd learned about fungi when researching her report—the way different fungi grew around roots and formed symbiotic relationships with trees. Mushrooms were the only part of fungi most people ever saw, but mushrooms were just the tip of the iceberg. Most of a fungus lived beneath the soil, just out of sight. Scientists were still studying the relationship between trees and fungi, and there was so much left to learn.

Suddenly Holly was overcome by a curiosity so strong she had to close her eyes and breathe through it. She wanted to understand the roots—to map them—to know how deep they went, and how they worked with the fungi. All she needed was time, she reasoned: quiet, uninterrupted time, free from the distraction of other people—

"DUCK!"

The warning came too late. The bouncy ball had already ricocheted off an arden tree and whacked Holly in the arm.

"Ow!" She whipped around to find the boy with the roller skates stomping through the tall grass toward her. "Just what do you think you're doing?"

"I'm Lionel."

"Just what do you think you're doing, Lionel?"

"Playing fetch. Also, saying hi." He paused. "Hi!"

"Fetch is for dogs," said Holly, snatching the bouncy ball out of a pile of leaves.

"I love dogs!" said Lionel. "It's pretty nice here, huh?" He opened his arms wide like he was giving the whole grove a hug. "When I was little, I used to come here every day and pretend to be Robin Hood. Or a werewolf. Or Leaf Man."

"Leaf Man?"

"A superhero I made up. He has leafy hair and vine fingers." Lionel snatched a yellow leaf that was drifting through the air and tucked it behind his ear.

Holly stared at the leaf, her annoyance at Lionel momentarily forgotten. She looked at the space between the roots, where fallen leaves littered the ground, then up at the canopy. There were red and yellow leaves mixed in with the green. "Is it normal for arden trees to drop leaves in early summer?" she asked.

Lionel scratched his head. "I dunno. I don't think so, now that you mention it. Hey, can you toss my ball back? We can play catch!"

Holly ignored him. She turned in a slow circle, looking from tree to tree, from root to crown. Now the whispering of the trees in the wind held a note of urgency. She felt an ache in her chest, the same ache she'd felt when she first laid eyes on Uncle Vincent's house. But this time she wondered if the ache was her own, or if it was coming from somewhere else—rising up through the ground, or drifting down from the canopy.

You're being silly, Holly Foster. You're getting carried away. She threw the bouncy ball back to Lionel and picked up the box of scones. "I was just leaving."

"Cool," said Lionel, pocketing the ball. "Me too!"

As Holly retraced her path through the trees, Lionel followed her. She grew more irritated with each crunch of his roller skates on the ground. Finally, she whipped around. "You know you're trampling those bushes, right?"

"Oops." He sidestepped over to where the ground was bare.

Holly sighed and marched out of the grove, trying to tune Lionel out. But when he reached the sidewalk, he was much more agile on his roller skates. Soon he was zooming past her down the street. "Hey, are those scones from Annie's? Those are sooooo good! They're freshest on Thursdays, that's when Annie—"

Lionel crashed into a streetlamp outside the factory and fell on his butt. A prim-looking woman walking down the street shook her head. "You *must* be more careful, Lionel."

"You got it, Ms. Dietrich!" Lionel said from the ground.

Ms. Dietrich squinted at Holly. Her hair was pulled back into a tight bun that seemed to stretch all the skin of her face. "You must be Vincent Foster's niece."

Holly nodded reluctantly. Her odds of remaining a stranger in Arden were looking slimmer by the moment. She already missed the grove. The pre-Lionel grove, to be specific. The feeling of being surrounded by trees and nothing and no one else.

While Ms. Dietrich pushed through the iron gates that guarded the factory grounds, Holly helped Lionel stand. "You really should be more careful. Why do you go around in roller skates if you don't know how to use them?"

"I just got 'em. I had a scooter but I busted it. Before that, I had a skateboard, but—"

"You busted that, too?"

"How'd you know?"

Holly rolled her eyes and kept walking down Cornelia Street, past Uncle Vincent's shop and Annie's Market.

Lionel skated more slowly beside her. It was quiet for a minute. Then Lionel started whistling. The tune was dreadfully chipper.

"Are you *always* this happy?" Holly asked.

"Not always. It's pretty lonely here, if you wanna know the truth."

Holly stared at him, startled. *Loneliness isn't something you talk about,* she thought. *It's only something you feel when you're all alone and nobody is watching and nobody has to know.* But Lionel said it like he was commenting on the weather.

"Most people in Arden are nice," he went on. "But there aren't a lot of kids my age. I go to school a few towns away, and none of my friends from school live here."

"Can't you visit them?"

"It would be far to roller-skate. Like, really far. Also, I can't drive. I'm eleven."

"Can't your parents drive you?"

Lionel seemed at a loss for words then, which Holly suspected didn't happen often. He stared at his roller skates, and Holly still felt annoyed, but now she felt guilty, too, which only made her more annoyed. "Or . . . can't your friends come visit you here?"

"I ask them to," Lionel said. "But they're busy. At least, that's what their parents say when I call. So I was thinking that you and I should be friends."

"Friends? I don't even know who you are."

"Lionel," said Lionel. "I've been waiting for you to get here ever since Mr. V said you were coming to stay with him. Mr. V is the best, so you must be the best, too."

"I'm not— I don't even know my uncle that well. And I get along fine without friends."

"Liar."

The guilt vanished. The annoyance swelled. Holly dug her heels into the sidewalk and glowered at Lionel. "What did you just call me?"

"Everyone needs friends. Otherwise you'll be lonely all the time. Won't you?"

Holly bristled. Sometimes she felt so lonely she couldn't breathe. But sometimes loneliness was a blanket—cold but familiar—and she curled up in it, made a nest inside it. "Why are you following me?"

"When your uncle told me you were coming to Arden, which was eight days ago, I started a countdown on my calendar. Eight days till Holly arrives. Then seven, then six, then—"

"Stop," said Holly, squeezing her eyes shut. When she opened them, she saw Lionel plucking an inchworm off his shirt and setting it on a bush.

"Should we give this little guy a name?" he said.

Yes, Holly thought. "No," she said. "Listen. I'm only going to be here for a month, and maybe not even that long. It might only be a couple weeks, or one week, or—"

She paused. How long would it take her dad to fall out of heaven this time?

"Then we can be friends for a month, or a couple weeks, or one week. Deal?"

"No. I mean . . . I don't know." Holly scrunched up her face. "My head hurts."

"That's what my dad always says."

Holly pointed up the street that led back to Uncle Vincent's. "I'm going that way. And you're going . . . some other way. Okay?"

Lionel shrugged. "If you say so. See you tonight!"

"Wait, what?" Holly said, but Lionel was already zipping away on his roller skates.

When he was out of sight, Holly found herself staring at the inchworm. Entirely against her will, a name popped into her head: Fitzwilliam.

"Ridiculous," Holly muttered, then carried on her way.

SIX

Holly sat on her bed and skimmed *Common Trees of the Eastern United States.* She was looking for trees that shed leaves in early summer instead of autumn. She couldn't find any.

Maybe it was normal for arden trees. After all, they weren't covered in her book, and they had other unique qualities—the shimmering bark, for one. But Lionel had said he didn't think the summer leaf loss was normal.

A prickly idea was taking root in Holly's mind: something was wrong with the arden trees.

It was just a hypothesis, she told herself. She would need evidence to confirm it. And the ache that she'd felt in the grove, the ache that she still felt in the center of her chest—that wasn't evidence. Was it?

A knock on her door made her jump. "What?" she snapped. "I mean, come in."

Uncle Vincent opened the door just enough to poke his head through. "Sorry to bother you. I just wanted to let you know that folks will be arriving soon for the Save the Grove meeting, and . . . Would you like to join? You don't have to. But if you want to . . ."

Holly felt a feeling she couldn't quite name. It was a little like the feeling she'd had with Lionel earlier—a mix of frustration and curiosity, and a kernel of hope she didn't understand.

"I think I'll stay up here," she said.

She saw the disappointment in Uncle Vincent's face—saw the way he covered it up fast, too. "Do you want any tea? Or scones?"

"No thanks." But then, as Uncle Vincent was about to close the door, she said, "Well . . . maybe a scone."

Uncle Vincent smiled.

When he went downstairs, Holly checked her phone. Her mom had sent a couple more pictures: Topher eating cheesecake in the cruise ship's dining hall; Ron leaning against the rail of the deck and smiling for the camera. There was a text, too: Did you get the toothpaste I sent?

Her dad had also sent a picture. He was standing outside a theater, pointing at a poster advertising the upcoming production of *A Midsummer Night's Dream.* First day of on-site rehearsals, he said. Wish me luck!

Holly took a picture of herself, then studied it. Her face was poorly lit by the bedside lamp and her always-bushy hair was more frazzled than usual. She thought about sending the picture to her parents. *I'm having the adventure of a lifetime, too. Just so you know.* Then she remembered what Annie had said at the market. *Vincent said you'd be coming to stay with him. My goodness, you two look just alike!*

She'd thought it was nonsense at the time. But now, looking at the picture, it occurred to her that she had high cheekbones like Uncle Vincent. She had his narrow nose and small mouth, too. And there was something about the eyes—not the color, exactly, or the shape, but something else that Holly couldn't put her finger on.

When Uncle Vincent knocked on her door again, she threw her phone down, embarrassed that she'd been comparing their faces. The doorbell rang as he set a plate down for her on the bedside table.

"If you'd like to just say hi to everyone," Uncle Vincent said, "or if you want more food . . ."

"I can come down. I know."

Uncle Vincent nodded. On his way out, he left her door open a crack.

Holly returned to her book, but soon the doorbell rang again, and again, and the sounds of chatter and laughter rose up and filled her tiny room. The wooden house creaked as it settled, and the air grew warm and maple-scented. Eventually Holly realized she'd been staring at the same paragraph in *Common Trees* for several minutes, seeing but not seeing.

She dropped the book and grabbed the plate. Uncle Vincent had brought her not one but two scones. She bit into one. It was delicious. Unreasonably delicious. Crisp and sugar-dusted and bursting with maple flavor.

For a while, she sat on the edge of the bed, a half-eaten scone in her hand. Her heart pitter-pattered. Her stomach growled. Everything felt ticklish.

Then, ever so quietly, she carried the plate of scones out of her room and took a seat on one of the highest stairs. From here, she could peek through the banisters and see the main floor of the house while remaining mostly hidden.

There were three people in the living room with Uncle Vincent. Holly was surprised to recognize two of them.

There was Annie, of course. She was lifting the lid off a casserole dish on the coffee table. "Spicy mac 'n' cheese! My secret family recipe."

"How spicy?" said an old woman sitting on the couch—the same old woman Holly had passed on the street that morning. Henry, the tortoise, lay by the woman's feet, slowly eating a piece of lettuce out of her hand. *I guess the tortoise really is her pet,* Holly thought.

"It's definitely got a kick," said Annie. "You'll like it, Beatrice!"

"You know you don't have to cook for these meetings, Annie," said Uncle Vincent.

"I know, I know." Annie slipped off her shoes and sat cross-legged on the couch. "I wanted to. Especially since I don't know how much longer . . ." Her sentence trailed away like one of Uncle Vincent's. "Oh, there I go again. Come on, eat up!"

The fourth Save the Grove Committee member was a man with light-brown skin and shoulder-length locs. He sat in a rocking chair, leaning forward, his chin resting on his clasped hands and his foot tapping the wood floor. He hadn't spoken yet, but there was a buzzy energy around him, like a hummingbird in flight.

"I suppose we can get started," Uncle Vincent said, "now that we're all here." He looked at the stairs. Holly shrank back into the shadows. "Annie, you said you have an update for us?"

"First of all, you'll never guess who came into the market today. Your niece had just stopped by, when lo and behold, Mr. Madison walks in with Elise and Ray!"

"So Charles Madison finally found the courage to walk amongst us ordinary townsfolk," said Beatrice. "When was the last time someone saw him out and about in Arden?"

"I know," said Annie. "He spends half his time at the

factory and the other half in his mansion on the hill. When he bought sandwiches for his kids, he said something about supporting local businesses."

"Pah!" said Beatrice. "The only local business in his mind is that factory."

"The Madisons *do* fund the arts center," said Uncle Vincent. "And a handful of other local businesses and events."

"That's just so they can see their name on everything," Beatrice retorted. "The Madison Arts Center. The Madison Wing of the library. Soon the whole town will be called Madison!"

"It's more than that," said the man in the rocking chair. His voice was warm but sharp. Each word crackled like firewood. "When they pour money into this town and make it a little shinier, it keeps their name clean. People are less likely to push back—or even notice—when they do something wrong."

"It's complicated," said Uncle Vincent, nodding. "I love the arts center, and the new library wing is beautiful. But I suspect you're both right. I think we can recognize the positive impacts the Madisons have on Arden while still holding them accountable. Annie, it sounded like you weren't finished?"

"Not quite," said Annie. "Later today, Nelly Dietrich stopped by the market for her weekly lottery ticket, and . . . Well, I don't want to start us off on a sour note, but Nelly said the Madisons have already applied for a permit to cut down the grove."

"Can we trust a thing Nelly says?" said Beatrice. "She works for the Madisons!"

"She doesn't want the grove torn down, either," said Annie.

"Then why isn't she here?" said Beatrice, jabbing a finger in the air.

"For a lot of people in Arden, it's tricky," said Uncle Vincent. "They might want to save the grove, but if they work for the factory, they can't rock the boat without risking their jobs."

"Money speaks," said the man in the rocking chair, his foot tapping away. "And in a town this small, you can't just hop from job to job."

"I've known Nelly since I was a little girl," said Annie. "In fact, she babysat me once! She's not one to make waves, but I think she's trying to help us."

As Holly munched on the scones, her mind worked to keep up. Ms. Dietrich—that was what Lionel had called the woman who told him to be careful on his roller skates when he crashed into a telephone pole outside the factory gates.

Holly imagined the four people in the living room as points on a map. Then she imagined a thread stretching from Annie to a new point: Nelly Dietrich. *Like a family tree,* Holly thought, *but for a town.* She thought of Uncle

Vincent's map of Arden, with its network of crisscrossing roads. She thought of the roots of the arden trees, spreading through the earth and intertwining. The ache in her chest grew a little achier.

In fifth grade, Holly had tried to make her own family tree. It was one of the assignment options for her class's unit on ancestry and culture. But her dad didn't know much about his extended family, which left lots of gaps on her tree, and her mom's relatives were mostly unfamiliar names to Holly—they lived far away and didn't keep in touch. Then there was her parents' divorce to deal with, and her mom's new family . . . In the end, the assignment had just frustrated Holly. She'd never turned hers in.

She shook the memory away and tuned back in to the meeting.

"If Nelly *was* telling the truth," said Beatrice, "we're in trouble. The Madisons have all the town councilmembers in their pockets."

"It's discouraging news," said Uncle Vincent. "But let's focus on steps we can take."

Holly was a little surprised to see her uncle leading the meeting—and more surprised that he seemed comfortable doing it. He spoke in his usual soft voice, his hands cupped around a mug of steaming tea, but his sentences weren't trailing away. He felt like the room's center of gravity, gently holding everyone in orbit. "How are preparations for next week's town hall meeting coming along?" he asked. "I reserved time for us on the town hall agenda."

"I ordered more Save the Grove pins to hand out at the meeting," said Annie, holding up a tote bag and giving it a jangle. "We can make swag bags!"

"Thanks, Annie," said Uncle Vincent. "Reggie, are you still planning to perform?"

The man in the rocking chair nodded. "I'm working on a new song. A song for the grove."

Reggie. The name tickled Holly's brain until she placed it. *Blue Jazz Expressions.* Reggie Summers lived in Arden, and he was sitting in her uncle's living room. A thrill ran through Holly. She'd never met a real musician before—one with a CD and everything.

"That's lovely, Reggie!" said Annie.

"I'm excited to hear it," said Uncle Vincent. "And that reminds me—I was thinking we might try a personal approach at this town hall meeting. Maybe we could each share a reason why the grove matters to us? For instance, I could share how it was a visit to the grove during my first trip to Arden that convinced me to move here."

"Oh, I love that idea!" said Annie. "I could tell everyone about the picnics my family had in the grove when I was young. Beatrice, what about you?"

Beatrice sniffed. "I wouldn't care to share anything personal."

Holly saw her uncle hide a smile. "Beatrice," he said, "how's your opinion piece for the *Arden Gazette* coming along?"

"Delayed," said Beatrice. "I was going to finish it today after I walked Henry, but then I wrote a letter to Mr. Madison instead—a letter telling him why he's a darn fool."

Uncle Vincent choked on his tea. "Letter writing can be effective, but perhaps we should—"

He was interrupted by a *thunk* on the living room window. Holly squinted through the banisters and saw Lionel's face pressed against the glass.

Beatrice grunted. "Not again. Tell that rascal to run along."

Annie wrung her hands together. "I hate to say it, but . . . Maybe we *shouldn't* let Lionel join this time, Vincent. Just in case."

Just in case what? Holly wondered.

Her uncle stood. "Anyone is welcome to the Save the Grove meetings." The firmness in his voice was another surprise to Holly.

When Uncle Vincent opened the front door, Lionel scurried inside. "Sorry I'm late!"

Annie forced a smile and Beatrice harrumphed, but Reggie greeted Lionel warmly with a fist bump. Holly felt a sting of jealousy. Lionel was friends with Reggie Summers?

"Help yourself to some food, Lionel," said Uncle Vincent.

Lionel swiftly obliged, fixing himself a plate of spicy mac 'n' cheese and maple scones. Then he sat on the couch next to Beatrice, who immediately scooted away from him. She squawked when her frail body sank into the crack between cushions.

"Now, where were we?" Uncle Vincent said, giving his beard a tug. "Ah, letter writing. Yes. Maybe we can focus on writing respectful letters to town councilmembers . . ."

As the meeting carried on, Lionel's eyes roamed the house. Holly knew, somehow, that he was looking for her. Her face burned. She was embarrassed that she was listening, embarrassed that she was eating scones, embarrassed that some small part of her—maybe even a medium-sized part of her—was happy to see Lionel.

She was relieved when Lionel turned his attention to Henry. He reached down to pat the tortoise's shell, much to Beatrice's annoyance. "He must have space when he eats," the old woman chided as she fed Henry another piece of lettuce. "Otherwise he gets a stomachache."

Holly stood in the shadows. She couldn't think of any reason to keep listening—in fact, she wasn't sure why she'd started listening in the first place. She tried to avoid the creaky stairs as she crept back up to the second floor, where solitude and books awaited her. Still, she heard the voices below.

"It sounds like we're on track for the town hall meeting," said Uncle Vincent. "Great work, everyone. Now, at our last committee meeting, we mentioned printing more yard signs—"

"It's not enough." The urgency in Reggie's voice made Holly freeze on the second-floor landing. "The pins, the yard signs, the town hall meeting—it's good, but it won't be enough. Things are in motion. These factory folks, they've started a wave. The wave is big, and it'll keep coming, and it'll hit. I've seen this kind of thing before in other towns. It just takes money and power, and they've got both. We're building a wave, too, but it's not big enough. Not yet. And we're running out of time."

The house fell silent. The only sound came from outside—the whistle of the wind through the birches. Holly's heart beat fast and strong as she stood on the landing, and there was the ache again, rising up from the earth, moving through the timbers of the house, burrowing beneath her skin. Except now the ache wasn't just an ache; it was a tug, pulling her downstairs.

Don't, she told herself. *It's none of your business. You'll leave soon and you'll never see these people again. You'll probably never step foot in Arden again. You'll forget all about this place, and this place will forget all about you, just like every other place you've ever been. Nothing lasts.*

But the ache kept tugging, and Holly's mind turned to

another Fundamental Truth: Adults don't always know more than kids (and sometimes they know less). Holly *knew* trees. And she wasn't sure how, exactly, but maybe knowing trees would help her uncle and his friends save the grove.

For a minute she stood frozen on the landing, jittery with indecision. Then, without consciously deciding to, she found herself turning around. She descended one step, then another, staring bewildered at her feet like they belonged to a stranger.

Soon she was at the bottom of the stairs, and everyone was turning toward her, and the house was holding its breath. Uncle Vincent, Annie, Lionel—they all smiled in their own ways. Reggie looked at her inquisitively while Beatrice blinked at her from behind enormous glasses. Even the tortoise craned his neck to stare at her, a piece of lettuce dangling from his mouth.

"Aren't you that girl who got in Henry's way this morning?" said Beatrice.

"I didn't get in anyone's—" She sighed. "I was just going to say, I did a science report on trees."

Suddenly she remembered visiting Chicago with her dad, years ago. They'd gone to a circus. She remembered how the spotlight had fallen on the tightrope walker. She felt a bit like that tightrope walker now.

"Tree root systems," she went on. "How roots grow, and

how they connect, and how they communicate with each other. Anyway, I went to the grove today, and I was thinking there might be an environmental case for saving the trees. If we knew more about the trees, and what makes them unique . . ." She paused, caught her breath, forged ahead. "I interviewed a forester for my science report. He fights to protect forests in Florida. He might have ideas. And he might know why the arden trees are losing so many leaves this early in the year. It's something I noticed today, and I don't think it's normal. So maybe you could reach out to him. Or . . ." She looked at her uncle. "I could email him. If you want. If that would be . . . helpful."

It was silent. The silence confused Holly—angered her and scared her, too. She felt the tightrope fraying.

Then Annie said, "I think that's a *wonderful* idea, Holly."

Reggie nodded. "It's fresh. We need fresh."

"I *knew* you would be smart," said Lionel. "I knew it before I even met you!"

Beatrice gave Holly a withering look, but even she said, "It can't hurt to try."

Uncle Vincent, meanwhile, rummaged through Annie's tote bag. Then he handed Holly a Save the Grove pin. "Welcome to the team," he said.

SEVEN

Holly woke early the next morning. She heard Uncle Vincent moving around downstairs. She heard him humming, too. This surprised her. She hadn't known her uncle was a hummer.

She buried her head under the pillow and tried to go back to sleep, but then she thought about her offer to email the forester she'd interviewed for her science report. She'd email him later, she decided, after more sleep and a leisurely morning. Yes—there was no rush.

But then she pondered what she'd say in the email. She started forming sentences in her head, and wondered if the forester would remember her, and what he would say, and— "Ugh!" she exclaimed. "I'll just do it now."

She drafted the email on her phone while she was still under the covers. She typed and erased, read and reconsidered, recast and rephrased . . .

. . . then hit Send.

Dear Mr. Kindale,

This is Holly Foster. You might not remember me, but I interviewed you for my sixth-grade science report. I hope it's okay that I'm emailing you again.

I'm staying with my uncle in a small town in Vermont called Arden. You probably haven't heard of it. It's kind of weird. But there's a grove of trees here that only grow in this area and nowhere else in the world. They're called arden trees.

A factory is trying to tear down the grove so they can build a visitors' center and museum. My uncle and some of his friends are trying to save the grove. I guess I'm trying to save the grove, too.

Do you have any advice? How do you save a grove? Also, do you know of any trees that shed lots of leaves in summer? I'm worried something might be wrong with the arden trees.

I look forward to hearing from you at your convenience.

Actually, I'm in a hurry, because I'm only visiting and

the factory is getting closer to destroying the grove. So I look forward to hearing from you ASAP.

Thank you,

Holly

Holly stared at her phone as she ate granola and drank black tea at Uncle Vincent's dining table. Her uncle had left for work and the house felt sleepy and still. Holly, on the other hand, was restless. It was perfectly reasonable for Dr. Kindale not to have responded yet, of course. It had hardly been an hour. But . . . *still.*

This was exactly why Holly didn't like reaching out to people. If they didn't respond right away, it felt like a rejection. (She tried not to think about the text from her classmate Abigail, still sitting unanswered on her phone.)

She didn't have to wait much longer, though. Shortly after breakfast, as Holly busied herself with scrolling through channels on her uncle's old, boxy TV, she received a reply from Dr. Kindale.

Hi, Holly! I remember you. How did that report turn out?

Sounds like the trees in Arden are pretty special. Has the town conducted an ecological assessment of the grove? If the grove is determined to have high environmental value, that might be enough to get protected status for it at a state or even a national level. An assessment might solve the mystery of that leaf loss, too.

Your best bet is to talk to someone familiar with that region's forests and ecology. I suggest reaching out to the forestry department at Vermont Technical Institute. Try to connect with Susan Morales. She's a professor there. I don't know her personally, but I heard her speak at a conference once. This might be up her alley.

Cheers,

Alan Kindale

Field Ecologist

Southeast Sustainable Forestry Advocates (SSFA)

Holly spent a good part of her day tracking down Susan Morales's email address on the Vermont Technical Institute website. She read about the institute's forestry program, too—an entire program dedicated to studying trees and forests. Holly's brain fizzed and hummed as she read about the program's classes, and the greenhouse on campus, and all the books about trees that the faculty had published. . . .

Until, finally, she closed her web browser and drafted her next email.

Dear Dr. Morales,

My name is Holly Foster. I found your email address on the Vermont Technical Institute website. My uncle is part of the Save the Grove Committee in Arden, Vermont. He and his friends are trying to save a grove of arden trees from being torn down by a plastics factory.

I think in order to save the grove we need to do an ecological assessment. At least, that's what a forester named Alan Kindale told me. He suggested I reach out to you. I don't know what an ecological assessment means, but maybe you do.

Can you help? Please?

Thank you,

Holly

As sunset filled Uncle Vincent's house with burnt-orange light, Holly paced the downstairs hallway, careful not to knock over any teetering stacks of books. Every few seconds she refreshed her email on her phone. Every time there wasn't a new message, she sighed louder. Dr. Morales wasn't as speedy as Dr. Kindale, it seemed.

Since Uncle Vincent had returned from work, he'd been sitting in the living room, painting a canvas on his tray table. When Holly's sighs got as loud as sighs can get, he paused his art tutorial DVD and said, "Everything okay?"

"Yes," said Holly. Before Uncle Vincent hit Play, she added, "I just don't know why Dr. Morales hasn't emailed me back yet!"

"Hmm . . . Let's see. When did you email her?"

"Five whole hours ago!"

A smile flickered across her uncle's face. "Waiting is hard. It can help to stay occupied."

"How?" *I don't want to sit on the couch and paint landscapes,* Holly thought, but she clamped her mouth shut before she could say it.

"Do you want to play that board game I picked up? I was reading the instruction manual earlier. It's a little complicated, but it could be fun . . ."

Holly tried to think of a way to tell him no that wouldn't bite. "Maybe some other time," she said slowly, which was code for: *I don't play games, especially board games, because they're silly and take too long and someone always cheats. Usually Dad.*

Uncle Vincent looked a little deflated, but a moment later he perked up. "Hey, why don't you come to my shop tomorrow? I have lots of documents and records from Arden's past. There's sure to be information about arden trees in there, too. I've been meaning to do some research myself, to see if there's anything that might help us save the grove."

The house creaked uncertainly. Holly deliberated. Even

though she was reaching out to foresters on behalf of the Save the Grove Committee, and even though she now had an official Save the Grove pin on her bedside table, she didn't know if she really wanted to be on the committee. She *couldn't* be on the committee, she reasoned, if she didn't live in Arden. And going to Uncle Vincent's shop to research Arden and the grove—that sounded like something a committee member might do. Someone who belonged to Arden. Someone who had reason to care what happened to the grove.

I'm just passing through, Holly told herself. *Not my town, not my business.* But the words were a little less comforting than she'd hoped.

"Of course," said Uncle Vincent, "you don't have to, if you don't want—"

"Fine. I'll come."

Uncle Vincent smiled. He nodded, and she nodded back. Then she resumed pacing while Uncle Vincent painted a lighthouse by the sea.

EIGHT

A soft bell chimed over Holly's head when she stepped into Uncle Vincent's shop the next morning.

Outside it was gray and drizzly, but inside it was warm. As she dried her shoes on the doormat, she inhaled the shop's scent—wood and leather and secrets and time. Then she walked narrow aisles of bookshelves, pausing to inspect titles along the way. There were vintage detective novels and children's encyclopedias; books on birding, books on growing herb gardens, and books on figuring out if your neighbor was a witch. (Apparently witches often had animal companions. Holly wondered if they ever had tortoises.) There were handcrafted objects for sale, too—ceramic bowls and antique glassware, wooden flutes and woven baskets.

She emerged from the maze of shelves and saw Lionel sitting behind the table at the back of the shop where she'd expected to find Uncle Vincent.

"Lionel! Where's my uncle?"

"Just a sec. I'm making a soufflé."

Holly frowned. Lionel was not making a soufflé. He was playing a game on his phone, squinting and sticking his tongue out the corner of his mouth in a look of fervent concentration.

Holly, meanwhile, checked her own phone. Still nothing from Dr. Morales.

Holly and Lionel sighed at the same time.

"The soufflé collapsed," he said. "It's a cooking game. Wanna try it?"

"No thanks."

"I have lots of other games. Racing games, spaceship games, fruit slicing games . . ."

"I don't play games. Where's—"

"Holly? Is that you?"

She followed the sound of her uncle's voice to a corner of the shop. A ladder led down from a trapdoor into a dim basement, where Uncle Vincent stood holding a stack of newspapers.

"What's all that?" Holly asked.

"Old editions of the *Arden Gazette*, the local newspaper." Uncle Vincent climbed the ladder and lowered the trapdoor behind him. "They date back to the mid-nineteenth century, when the *Gazette* was founded. I thought we could take a look. Newspapers are a good way to learn about the history of the town. Maybe the grove, too."

He cleared space on his worktable and set the newspapers down. "Oooh!" said Lionel, grabbing the paper on top of the stack.

"Are your hands clean, Lionel?" Uncle Vincent asked lightly.

"Yep! Just washed 'em."

"It's best to have clean, dry hands when working with old documents to prevent the oils in our fingers from damaging the paper," Uncle Vincent explained to Holly.

"Preserving stuff is a big part of being an antiquarian," said Lionel matter-of-factly.

Uncle Vincent nodded. "That's right, Lionel."

Holly looked from her uncle to Lionel, wondering if anyone was going to address the Lionel-shaped elephant in the room. "I'm sorry, but what are you doing here, Lionel?"

"I come here sometimes when school is out and everything is boring," said Lionel. "Or rainy."

"Lionel has taken an interest in antiquarianism," said Uncle Vincent. There was a hint of pride in his voice.

"Of course he has," Holly muttered. She wiped her hands on her jeans, sat down next to Lionel, and began sifting through the newspapers. Some of them were protected in large plastic sleeves, but she could still read the front pages. "What are we looking for, exactly?"

"Anything about the grove, I think," said Uncle Vincent. "Beyond that, it's hard to say. Sometimes we don't know what we're looking for until we find it."

Holly wanted to protest—how could she look for something if she didn't know what the something was?—but then Uncle Vincent's phone rang and he stepped into a small closet-turned-office, leaving Holly and Lionel with the newspapers.

"I'll take these," said Lionel, grabbing the top half of the stack. "Bet I find something about the trees before you do!"

"It's not a race," Holly chided. Still, she flipped through the papers quickly, her eyes darting from old dates to old headlines. *Blizzard to Hit the Northeast* read one from the 1940s, while a paper from the 1970s proclaimed *Vermont Senate Candidates to Visit Arden.*

For a while, nothing grabbed Holly's attention. She glanced at Lionel to make sure he wasn't faring any better. It wasn't a race, but if it was, she planned on obliterating him. So when Lionel said, "Whoa!" Holly shouted, "No!" She coughed and composed herself. "I mean, what did you find?"

"It's not about the trees," he said, "but look!"

Lionel's newspaper was dated April 15, 2009. The front-page headline read:

Hometown Girl Annie Furr Opens
Market on Cornelia Street

In a photo, a younger-looking Annie stood in front of the market, smiling broadly. Holly and Lionel put their heads together and scanned the article, which continued on page seven.

> *"Food brings people together," Ms. Furr says of her new business venture. "I've loved cooking and baking ever since my grandma taught me how to roll dough when I was a little girl. Annie's Market is a place where I can share some of my own creations—and other delicious food—with this town I love so much."*

"Wait," said Holly. "Does Annie make those maple scones herself?"

"Yup. She bakes them fresh every Thursday. That's what I was trying to tell you before I ran into that telephone pole the other day." Lionel pointed to another article on page seven and giggled. "Look at the opinion column."

A Case for Honey Mustard
by Beatrice Quill

> *My husband and I just moved to Arden last month, but I've already noticed countless deficiencies in this town.*

Perhaps none are so troubling as the lack of honey mustard in Arden restaurants. Everybody knows that honey mustard is the preferred condiment for French fries, far superior to ketchup (dreadful) and regular mustard (unspeakable). Its absence is a discredit to this town and its cuisine. . . .

Uncle Vincent returned from his call and glanced at the paper. "Beatrice has been speaking her mind ever since she arrived," he said with a chuckle.

"I didn't know she was married," said Holly.

"Her husband passed away a few years back."

"Oh," said Holly, feeling awkward for bringing it up and more awkward for not knowing what to say next. She folded the newspaper and set it aside. In a businesslike voice, she said, "Let's start a stack of papers that we might want to come back to. We still need to find something about the grove."

"You got it, boss," said Lionel.

Holly allowed herself a smile. It was nice to be called boss. But her thoughts soon turned back to Beatrice. She imagined taking the old woman's hand in hers and giving it a reassuring squeeze—then wondered where on earth that idea had come from.

Morning turned to afternoon as they pored through the newspapers. When Uncle Vincent wasn't taking calls or working at his laptop, he brought up more papers from the basement and helped sort through them. All the while, the rain picked up, drumming on the roof and streaking down the windows that looked out on Cornelia Street. Holly saw people hurrying by on the sidewalk, umbrellas held aloft and raincoats flapping in the wind.

Holly loved the rain. She loved its sweet, earthy smell and the symphony of sounds it made as it hit different surfaces, from tinny pings to deep roars. She loved, too, the way rain fed trees, water soaking into soil so roots could drink it up and send it through the trunk to every branch. Something about being dry and cozy in Uncle Vincent's shop while knowing that the grove was being nourished by the rain made Holly feel peaceful. It was a feeling she often had when she was in nature, but she wasn't used to feeling it indoors—or around other people.

"Hey, this one is about the grove!" said Lionel. He'd found mention of a winter frost that killed several arden trees in 1962. Shortly after, Uncle Vincent found a 1916 article about a family of owls that had taken up residency in the grove.

They added both papers to their special stack, along with a paper Holly found from the summer of 1924 announcing the town's first-ever Midsummer festival—a celebration to be held in the grove on Midsummer's Eve, complete with food, live music, and dancing. The festival's name made

Holly think of *A Midsummer Night's Dream.* The image came to her unbidden: her dad prancing through the grove as Woodland Sprite #4. She suppressed a giggle.

"Is this festival still a thing?" she asked.

"Hmm," said Uncle Vincent, taking a look at the article. "No, I haven't heard of this. Lionel, what about you?"

"Nope," said Lionel. "It sounds fun, though!"

"If it was an annual festival, it must have stopped many years ago," said Uncle Vincent. "It's an interesting find, though."

An interesting find. Holly felt pleased with herself.

When their stomachs began to rumble, Uncle Vincent put on his raincoat and left them in charge of the shop while he fetched a late lunch. Holly was alarmed—she didn't know how to run an antiquarian shop—but Lionel told her not to worry. "It's easy. If any customers come in, just look smart but quiet, like an old wizard." Lionel made an expression that looked eerily like Uncle Vincent. This time, Holly didn't manage to suppress her giggle. Lionel's face lit up as she laughed.

Uncle Vincent returned quickly with sandwiches and cookies from Annie's. "Did I miss anything?"

"We sold everything and made you a billion dollars," said Lionel.

"Well, then, I should've picked up more cookies!"

Holly felt a pinprick of jealousy. Uncle Vincent and

Lionel got along so easily. But *she* was his niece. Shouldn't *she* be the one bantering with him? Not that she cared much for banter. She shooed away the feeling and reached for one of the wrapped sandwiches.

Before she unwrapped it, the edge of a headline caught her eye. She tugged a plastic-covered paper out from the bottom of the stack. This one was dated February 1, 1898.

Section of Arden Forest to Be Cut Down as Industrialist Thomas Madison Promises Progress

"Thomas Madison," Holly said. "That must be . . ."

Uncle Vincent and Lionel exchanged a look. "Charles Madison's great-great-grandfather," said Uncle Vincent. "He opened the factory."

Holly looked at the black-and-white photograph of Thomas Madison beneath the headline. With his top hat and mustache, he looked a lot like how Holly had imagined Charles Madison before she saw him in Annie's Market.

She scanned the article. It was hard to read—the ink was smudged and the language was old-fashioned—but she learned that the grove of arden trees had once been large enough to be considered a forest. Over half of it had been cleared to make way for the existing factory.

"So the Madisons already destroyed most of the grove, and now they want to get rid of the only part left." She looked at Lionel and was annoyed to find him staring off into space, like a robot that had been powered off. She turned to Uncle Vincent. "This is important, isn't it? If we can remind everyone that the factory has already cut down lots of trees, we—I mean, *you*—can stop them from doing it again, right?"

Uncle Vincent looked from Lionel to Holly. She couldn't read his face. "Maybe," he said. "It's certainly good information to have."

"Well, *I* think it's important." She placed the newspaper on top of the special stack, then unwrapped her sandwich and inspected it. "Um. Are those olives?"

"Mm-hmm," said Uncle Vincent. "A Mediterranean sandwich. One of Annie's specialties. Is . . . that okay?"

"Olive oil is good but olives are gross," Holly announced. "It's one of the Fundamental Truths of Life."

Worry swam across her uncle's face. "Oh, I didn't realize . . ."

"It's a what kind of truth of life?" Lionel asked.

"Fun-da-men-tal," Holly said. "That means it's really, *really* true, and it's always been true, and it always will be true."

Lionel looked like he was thinking hard. "But I love olives."

"Well, they're *my* Fundamental Truths. They're true for *me*."

Uncle Vincent's expression turned inquisitive. "How did you come up with your fundamental truths?"

"And what are the others?" said Lionel.

Holly squirmed. She didn't usually tell people about her Fundamental Truths. In fact, she wasn't sure why she'd brought them up at all. "Never mind," she said.

"Well, I'm sorry about the sandwich. . . ." Uncle Vincent began.

"It's fine," Holly said. But it wasn't, not really. When Uncle Vincent wasn't looking, she opened the sandwich and picked out all the olives and set them on a napkin. She knew the hint of olive flavor would linger, briny and terrible, but she did what she could.

"So you're not going to eat those?" Lionel whispered, looking meaningfully at the napkin. Holly slid it over to him. Then she took small bites of the sandwich—the olive flavor did linger, but it wasn't *too* terrible—and looked around the shop. It occurred to her that there hadn't been a single customer all day. Lionel had joked that they'd sold everything, but in reality they hadn't sold anything.

"Where are all the customers?" she asked. Then she wondered if the question was rude.

Her uncle didn't seem bothered, though. "Most of my customers don't live in Arden. Everything here is listed on the shop's website. Sometimes people travel to Arden to visit the shop, but it's more common for collectors around the world to order online or by phone. That's how I do most of my business."

"Who are the collectors? What are they collecting?"

"Lionel, do you want to take that question?"

Lionel tossed an olive in his mouth. Holly shuddered. "It depends," he said. "Different people are looking for different things."

"That's right," said Uncle Vincent. "The phone call I took earlier was from a woman who collects Civil War documents."

"Do you have any?" Holly asked.

"A few. But none that mention her ancestor—a Union Army general. Some people just want a piece of history. Others want a piece of their personal history."

Holly looked around the shop again, wondering how many secrets it held. How many family trees had roots that ran through Uncle Vincent's books and documents and antiques? Was it easier for people from small towns to make family trees, especially if their family had lived in the same town for generations?

The ache in Holly's chest flared up. *Staying in one place would be boring*, she thought. *I get to go lots of different places and see lots of different things that most people never see.* And she felt a little better. Just a little.

Then she ate the chocolate-chip cookie from Annie's and felt *much* better. It was the best cookie she'd ever eaten—better than the giant cookie she'd had from a New York City food truck, and better than the cookies her neighbor in Winter Park had baked to welcome her and her dad to the neighborhood. She didn't tell Uncle Vincent and Lionel this, though.

Lionel burped. "I'm tired of looking at newspapers."

"It's been a full day," said Uncle Vincent. "You two did good work."

Holly looked at their special stack of newspapers with pride. Then she realized that she hadn't opened her email in a couple hours. Where had the time gone? She brushed cookie crumbs off her hands and checked her phone. There was an email waiting for her.

Holly,

Thanks for reaching out. As a matter of fact, I have a couple of students who are looking for a summer research project. Assessing the arden trees might just be a fit for them.

They can visit the grove on Friday morning. I'll join if I can. You're welcome to join, too. Let me know a good phone number to reach you so we can coordinate.

Best,

Susan Morales, PhD

Forestry Department

Vermont Technical Institute

Holly tried to sound casual as she read the email aloud, but her voice shook with excitement.

"Wonderful news!" said Uncle Vincent.

"So cool!" said Lionel. "Can I come, too?"

"We can all go," said Uncle Vincent. "I can open the shop late on Friday."

Holly exhaled. She'd been worried that Dr. Morales might not respond—that she was too busy, or that Holly's email was silly and unimportant. But Dr. Morales *had* responded. And she was coming to Arden on Friday.

Friday. The day after tomorrow. So soon but so far.

Holly emailed Dr. Morales her phone number, then checked her texts. There was a new batch of cruise ship photos from her mom and a reminder to use her prescription toothpaste. From her dad, a picture of him in his Woodland Sprite #4 costume. He had a flower crown on his head and his arms were wreathed in fake vines and plastic butterflies. Full costume rehearsal, he'd texted. Show opens Friday. The guy playing Lysander has a cough. I bet he'll get a cold and need to miss some shows—maybe even opening night! Then: How's Vinny's? Need a rescue mission?

Holly considered this. She listened to the rain on the roof. She looked from Uncle Vincent to Lionel. She replayed Dr. Morales's email in her mind.

I'm fine, she texted back, shielding her phone so her uncle

couldn't see her dad's message. It was what she always said when people asked how she was doing, but this time, she had the strange feeling that she almost meant it.

Before she put her phone away, the text from Abigail caught her eye. *Hi, Holly! How's your summer going?* Holly's fingers hovered over the touch-screen keyboard . . .

. . . then she pocketed her phone. "What do we do until Friday?" she asked. She imagined holing up in her room until then, reading her nature books. It was exactly what she'd planned on doing for her entire time in Arden, but it didn't feel quite right anymore. Reggie Summers was right: time was ticking for the grove. She might not be an official Save the Grove Committee member, and she might have to leave in a month—less than a month now—but as long as she was here . . .

"There's still work we need to do to prepare for the town hall meeting next Thursday," said Uncle Vincent. "Why don't you see if any of the other Save the Grove Committee members could use a hand?"

"Or four hands," said Lionel.

"Four?" said Holly.

He wiggled his fingers. "Your two hands and my two hands."

Holly wanted to tell Lionel that she'd had quite enough of his company, but his wiggling fingers made her laugh.

That was two Lionel-inspired laughs in one day. Maybe she could tolerate his presence for a little longer.

She adopted a businesslike voice again. "Lionel, meet me at Annie's Market tomorrow morning at ten o'clock."

"You got it, boss!"

NINE

A timid sun shone down on Arden on Thursday morning. The streets glistened from overnight rain and dogs splashed in puddles in the town square.

Holly found Lionel waiting for her outside Annie's Market. He was crouching by a tuft of grass sprouting through a sidewalk crack. "Look!" he said. "D'you think it's the same worm from the other day?"

Holly crouched beside him and spotted the inchworm inching along a blade of grass. "Fitzwilliam?"

"So you *did* name him."

"It's probably not the same one," Holly said gruffly. "I'm sure there are lots of inchworms here."

"Yeah," said Lionel. "But maybe?"

"Maybe," Holly conceded.

She stood and saw that the Now Hiring sign on the market window was wet and crumpled from the rain. She smoothed it out and retaped it to the glass, then entered the shop with Lionel. He sniffed the air and grinned. "Thursday. Baking day."

Annie bustled through a saloon-style door at the back of the market, wiping her flour-dusted hands on her apron. "Morning! What can I do for you two? Shopping for Vincent?"

Holly told Annie about Dr. Morales and the forestry students coming to inspect the grove on Friday. "I didn't know what to do till then, so . . . Is there anything we can do to help you prepare for the town hall meeting next week? If you don't need help, that's fine. You don't *have* to need help. Lionel and I can leave if—"

"Oh my gosh. I would *love* help. It's sweet of you to offer. And how exciting about the foresters! Now, let's see. On Thursdays, I whip up all the baked goods that I sell throughout the week, and this afternoon I'm interviewing someone. I just don't know when I'm going to get to those." Annie nodded at a stack of cardboard boxes behind the register. Holly lifted the flaps of the top box. Inside were bundles of pencils and stickers.

"Save the Grove swag," Annie explained. "We want to hand out things at the town hall meeting to help people stay connected to the issue and raise awareness. There should be tote bags in those boxes, too. Each bag gets a pin, a sticker, a pencil, and a chocolate-chip cookie. Could you two could assemble the bags? I have cookies cooling now, so we can add those last."

"We're on it!" said Lionel.

"Wonderful!" Annie checked her watch and sniffed the air. "I hope those croissants aren't burning . . . I'll leave you to it."

Annie pushed through the swinging door at the back of the shop. Holly followed her and peeked inside. The kitchen was small and bright, painted in shades of green and pink and yellow. Cookies and pies cooled on racks and mixing bowls were strewn about the counter. Holly watched for a minute, entranced, as Annie churned through the kitchen—checking the oven, stirring bowls, rolling dough, humming a frantic tune.

When Holly returned to the register, Lionel smiled devilishly. "Bet I can put more bags together than you."

Holly was about to remind Lionel that she didn't play games. But she was still sore about Lionel being the first to find a newspaper of interest at Uncle Vincent's shop yesterday. So she looked him in the eye and said, "Game on."

They tore open the boxes and made fast work of the swag: place a pin and a sticker and a pencil into a tote bag, repeat. Holly lost her breath trying to keep up with Lionel. "You're sitting closer to the bags," she panted. "That's not fair."

"You're sitting closer to the stickers," said Lionel. "Plus, you have long arms."

Holly looked at her arms, wondering if they were abnormally long. "Do not."

"Do too."

Holly narrowed her eyes. Lionel stuck out his tongue.

It was a race to the finish, but soon everything was sorted. They tallied up: eighteen swag bags for Lionel, nineteen for Holly. "Well," said Holly. Games were still silly, of course, but they were less silly when she won them.

"I put the pin in your nineteenth bag, so we both worked on that one. Call it a tie?"

"Ugh. Fine."

She took a closer look at the tote bags. They sported a different image than the Save the Grove pins and the yard signs around town. Here, the words *Save the Grove* were suspended in a cloud, floating over a forest. "Did Uncle Vincent design this, too?"

"He sure did," said Annie, carrying boxed pies to a table at the front of the market. "Your uncle is quite the artist! He also designed these flyers." She picked up a stack of papers from the counter by the register and handed them to Holly. The flyers advertised the town hall meeting—now one week away—and encouraged people to come make their voices heard on behalf of the grove.

"Since you two sorted those bags so quickly," said Annie,

"maybe you'd like to hang up some of these flyers around town? It's turning into a beautiful day after all that rain."

"Yeah!" said Lionel. "And I can give Holly the Arden Official Tour at the same time."

"There's an Arden Official Tour?" said Holly.

"Yep. I just made it up in my head."

"That's not official," Holly mumbled, but Lionel didn't seem to hear. And anyway, Holly liked the idea of being outside while the world still smelled like rain.

Annie handed them the flyers, a stapler, and tape. "You two are lifesavers. Come back for lunch, okay? My treat."

Holly stepped out into the late-morning sun with Lionel just as a family with three little kids entered the market. Before the door shut behind them, Holly heard Annie say, "Hi, Mary and Harry! Hi, August, Simone, and Max!"

"Does everyone here know everyone else's name?" Holly asked Lionel.

"I guess so," said Lionel. "Is that weird?"

"Yes. Well . . . I don't know. I've never visited a town this small. When we lived in Boston, my dad and I didn't even know our neighbors' names."

"But that's so sad," said Lionel.

"It's not *sad*," said Holly.

Lionel shrugged. "If you say so. Okay, the Arden Official Tour begins . . . now!"

Holly had to power walk to keep up with Lionel as he

scampered through downtown Arden. He talked as fast as he moved, offering a running commentary on everything they passed. "This is the town square. Sometimes musicians play here, like Reggie Summers. He's my favorite musician ever, and also one of my favorite friends ever. See that bench? It's dedicated to Madeline Jones. I don't know who Madeline Jones is, but one time I stubbed my toe on that bench and it hurt a lot.

"See that building over there? It used to be a theater, and then it was a candy store, and now it's Mr. Butler's Cat Massage Parlor—"

"Mr. Butler's *what*?"

"A massage parlor for cats. Your town doesn't have one of those? They never took down the theater sign, and it still smells like licorice inside. And that fire hydrant—it's an Arden tradition that when you adopt a dog, you bring it to the hydrant so it can pee on it. Sometimes crowds gather to watch the dog's first hydrant pee. I want a dog but my mom won't let me get one. She says she's allergic but I don't believe her, unless being allergic to dogs means you just don't like dogs."

Holly stuck flyers on a notice board in town square, on a broken marquee by the theater-turned-candy-shop-turned-cat-massage-parlor, and on a streetlamp next to the fire hydrant. Part of her wanted Lionel to keep talking, to tell her everything about everything. But part of her wanted him to stop, because the more he talked, the more she felt a creeping sadness. She'd never known any place the way Lionel knew Arden. She wondered what it felt like to live in the same town your whole life, to have a memory tied to every bench and hydrant. *Boring*, she thought. But she wasn't sure. And she didn't like not being sure. That was why it was good to have Fundamental Truths.

She repeated the Truths mentally to herself. Then, when Lionel paused to catch his breath, she said, "I've lived in Virginia and Texas and Massachusetts and Florida. And I've visited a lot more places, like New York City and Las Vegas. The Grand Canyon, too."

She was pleased to see Lionel's jaw drop. "Really? That's so cool! I've never even left Vermont."

Holly went on breezily: "I've also been to Chicago. I went to the very top of this really tall skyscraper. There was an area where the floor was glass and it felt like I was flying over the city. I saw a circus show there, too. There were acrobats and people who juggled torches. . . ."

As she spoke, it occurred to Holly that she'd never told anyone about her trip to Chicago—or any of her trips, really. The more she shared with Lionel, the more she felt exposed. Was it any of Lionel's business? Why should he care, anyway?

But Lionel was a rapt audience. His face lit up with wonder and delight at each new detail, and he wanted to know more. "Were you scared at the top of the skyscraper? How *big* is a skyscraper? A hundred stories? A thousand? Did you throw a pebble into the Grand Canyon? Are there alligators in Florida? Do they eat kids? Would they eat *me*?"

And Holly could answer his questions, because she'd really been to all these places. She'd really seen all these things, even if it was only because her dad dragged her along. And the creeping sadness was still there, but now it was mingled with pride, which . . . Well, it was confusing.

As they passed a florist shop, Holly decided she'd shared more than enough for one day. Maybe for a lifetime. "Let's ask the florist if we can give them some flyers to hand out," she said. But before she opened the shop door, Lionel grabbed her arm and dragged her behind a sunflower display.

"Lionel! What are you—"

"Shh!" He clamped a hand over her mouth, and they huddled in silence behind the sunflowers as a tall woman in a wide-brimmed hat walked down the sidewalk. The woman was on her phone. "I told you my car is having engine problems. Why didn't you wait for me? Now I'm having to walk through town in the heat. . . ."

"Who is that?" Holly whispered, prying Lionel's hand off her face. "And why are we hiding from her?"

"We're not hiding. I just . . . thought I saw a spider. Crawling on you. Or, about to crawl on you. But it's gone now. Whew!"

The woman was gone now, too. Holly glared at Lionel and plucked a sunflower petal out of his hair. *This would all be so much easier if I were doing it alone*, she thought.

She took charge then, marching down streets and hanging flyers while Lionel followed and chattered on about this and that and the other thing—a TV show about superheroes, his action figure collection, how he was giving his roller skates a break because he'd accidentally run into someone yesterday on his way home from Uncle Vincent's shop.

When they ran out of flyers, they returned to the market, where Annie was waiting for them with caprese sandwiches and iced teas. Holly was relieved to see that the sandwiches contained zero olives—just tomatoes, basil, and mozzarella cheese.

"I put the cookies in the bags, so we're all set with swag," Annie said while they ate. "Maybe I'll bake some lasagnas for the town hall meeting, too. . . ."

It might've been the deliciousness of the sandwich or her tiredness from all the flyer distribution, but when Holly's curiosity stirred, she didn't bother fighting it. "At the Save the Grove meeting, you said the market might not be around much longer."

Annie sighed. "That's right. My mom is in a care facility in Burlington. My dad is there, too. He got an apartment so he could see her every day, but lately he hasn't been doing so great, either. So . . ." Annie tidied a shelf of maple syrup jars. "I'm going to move there. At least for a little while."

"Move to *Burlington*?" Lionel spluttered. "But you can't! You're one of my favorite people in Arden. Definitely top five. And . . ." A look of dread washed over him. "Who's going to make maple scones if you're gone?"

Annie laughed and knuckled her eyes. "Lord, look at me, crying again. I'm trying to hire someone to take over the market while I'm gone so I don't have to close it. But there haven't been many bites. The only people who move to Arden come here to work at the factory, not a market."

"But you said you're interviewing someone," said Holly.

Annie nodded. "The other tricky thing is . . . I'm very *particular*. This market means a lot to me. It's hard to imagine leaving it with someone else."

Holly remembered the picture in the *Arden Gazette* from the market's opening day. *Hometown Girl Annie Furr Opens Market on Cornelia Street.* Fifteen years hadn't changed Annie's smile, but there were stress lines on her face now and a heaviness in her eyes.

"What made you want to open the market in the first place?" Holly asked.

"Gosh, it seems so long ago now! I left Arden for college and got a business degree. I didn't know what to do with it, but I've always loved making food. So I thought, why not open my own market?"

"But why *here*?" Holly pressed. "If you left Arden for school, why'd you come back?"

Annie looked thoughtful. "My older sister couldn't wait to get out of here. She said Arden was a nowhere town. But I always knew I'd come back. I still live in the house I grew up in, you know. It's a little different these days because it's just me. It's weird, the way the house echoes now."

For a moment they were quiet. Annie's eyes glistened. "I just hope I can do my part to help the grove before I leave. My family used to picnic in the grove every Sunday when I was little, you know. Pasta salad, crackers with brie, buttered rolls with grandma's homemade blueberry jam . . . I can still taste them! Now, my family was *loud.* Lots of talkers. But there was always a moment, after we'd eaten until we were stuffed and chatted about everything under the sun, that we'd all get really quiet. We'd listen to the birds, and the squirrels, and the trees. . . . That grove meant a lot to my family. It means a lot to *me.*" She smoothed out her apron. "Oh, enough of all that. How are the sandwiches?"

"Good," said Holly.

"Epic," said Lionel.

Holly frowned at Lionel for one-upping her with his word choice, then checked her phone for the time. It was early in the afternoon. There was a lot of day left to fill. "Is there anything else we can do to help you?"

"You've done plenty," said Annie. "Take the rest of the day off and relax!"

"I'm not very good at relaxing," said Holly.

Annie laughed. "You and me both. Well, let's see—you could check in with Reggie or Beatrice. Maybe they could use some help, too."

"I don't think Beatrice likes me," said Holly.

"That's okay," said Lionel. "Beatrice doesn't like anyone."

"That's not true and you know it, Lionel," Annie chided gently. "Beatrice can be a little prickly, but she has a good heart."

"Like you!" said Lionel, bumping his shoulder into Holly's.

"I am *not* prickly," said Holly, but she heard the prickle in her voice. She huffed. Sometimes she exasperated herself. She swallowed the last bite of her caprese sandwich, finished her iced tea, and stood.

"Where to, boss?" said Lionel.

"*I'm* going to see if Reggie needs any help. *You* can do whatever you want. Except . . . I don't know where Reggie lives."

"Next stop on the Arden Official Tour," said Lionel. "Reggie's place!"

TEN

Holly followed Lionel down Cornelia Street and across the town square to Miss Maisie's Wig Emporium. "Reggie lives *here*?" she said.

"Above the shop," said Lionel.

While Holly looked up at the small building's second story, Lionel poked his head through the door of the wig emporium. "Hi, Miss Maisie!"

"Good afternoon, Lionel," Miss Maisie cooed. Today she wore a curly silver wig with matching eye shadow. "Is that a friend of yours?"

"No," said Holly, but she was drowned out by a much louder "Yes!" from Lionel.

"Isn't that nice," said Miss Maisie. "New relationships form while others fall into the abyss. Why, I just heard that

Mr. Butler and Mr. Wilson broke up! It's all *very* shocking, but I'm not one to gossip. No, you didn't hear it from me! Now, are you two in the market for wigs today? I have *just* the thing for each of you."

"Not right now," said Lionel. "Just saying hi! Also, bye." He closed the door and ran around the side of the building. Holly followed him into an alleyway.

"Mr. Butler is the cat massage parlor guy, right?" she asked.

"Yup," said Lionel. "That's a bummer about him and Mr. Wilson. I thought that was true love for sure."

A van was parked in the alley beside metal stairs leading to a second-floor entrance. Lionel scurried up to the landing and pressed an ear to the door. "Reggie's playing something," he whispered.

Holly pressed her ear to the door, too. "Guitar?"

"Mandolin," Lionel replied knowingly. When there was a break in the music, he gave the door a loud knock. Holly's heart thumped. She'd already met Reggie at Uncle Vincent's house but now she was standing on his doorstep. What if Reggie Summers—*the* Reggie Summers—didn't like her? Or worse: What if he didn't think she was cool?

Reggie looked relieved when he opened the door. "Thought it was Miss Maisie complaining about the noise again," he said.

"We're here to help you get ready for the town hall meeting," Lionel announced.

"Yeah," said Holly, in her coolest, most unintimidated-by-anyone voice. "Annie said maybe you could use some help."

Reggie quirked an eyebrow. Even as he stood in the doorway, he was in motion: bare feet tapping, fingers drumming on the doorknob, head nodding to music only he could hear. "Not sure I need help for the meeting, but you're welcome to hang out. I'm laying down tracks."

"Cool," said Holly. "I mean . . . Sure, we can hang out." Then, like she was someone who always hung out with musicians, she followed Reggie and Lionel into a small, one-room apartment, barely bigger than Holly's room at Uncle Vincent's.

Besides a sofa bed, a tiny kitchenette, and a few suitcases, the apartment looked like a recording studio. Well, Holly had never *seen* a recording studio before, but Reggie's apartment was how she imagined one might look. There were instruments everywhere: a keyboard, a drum kit, and something guitar-like that Holly guessed was a mandolin, among others. There were microphones, too, and a machine with dials and blinking lights. Wires ran between everything, connecting the mics and instruments to the dial board, and the dial board to a laptop computer propped on a window ledge overlooking the town square.

Sunlight shone through the window and pooled at Holly's feet.

"You live here? Like . . . only here?" Holly immediately regretted the question. Why was being polite so hard? Why were *words* so hard? Now Reggie definitely wouldn't think she was cool.

But Reggie just laughed. "It's a little tight, isn't it? I've been pretty nomadic for the last few years, driving around the country and living out of my van. But when I decided to stick around Arden for a bit, I figured I'd better find a place, and this fit the bill."

"Whatcha recording today?" Lionel asked.

"The song I wrote for the grove. I'll play it live at the town hall meeting, but I want to get a recording of it, too. I'm still figuring out a few parts."

"How is it a song for the grove?" Holly asked. She felt like she was interviewing a rock star, which was a very bold thing to do.

Reggie stepped nimbly over the crisscrossing wires and adjusted one of the mics. "It's hard to explain. Places give you feelings. Sometimes I try to turn those feelings into sounds." He looked from Lionel to Holly. "You two have any music recording experience?"

They shook their heads.

"I went to a concert once with my dad, though," said Holly.

"And we're fast learners," said Lionel. "The fastest, probably."

Holly squinted at Lionel. How did *he* know if she was a fast learner? He barely knew her.

"Perfect," said Reggie. "I've got jobs for you." He put Lionel in charge of the laptop. "I'll give the signal when I'm ready for you to start the recording. All you have to do is click here."

"Roger that," said Lionel.

"Your task is a little trickier," Reggie told Holly. He sat her down at a stool by the board of dials and blinking lights. "This is a mixer. These dials control how much of each type of sound is fed into the recording software as I play." He showed her how to adjust the dials for treble—the higher-pitched sounds—and bass—the lower-pitched sounds. "As I play, listen through these headphones. If it starts to sound too tinny, turn down the treble and turn up the bass. If it starts to sound too heavy, turn down the bass and turn up the treble. Got it?"

"Um," said Holly.

"It's delicate. Sometimes the smallest adjustment is all you need. Gentle hands, yeah?"

"Gentle hands," Holly echoed, hoping Reggie didn't see that her hands were quivering. Lionel gave Holly a grin and a thumbs-up. Holly gulped.

Reggie picked up the mandolin, gave Lionel the signal,

and began playing. The sound poured into Holly's ears through the headphones: a bright, rollicking rhythm. Holly tried to trace the path of the sound. Reggie's fingers moved across the fretboard and strings, bringing the instrument to life. The music fed into a microphone and ran through wires into her mixing board and headphones, then through more wires until it appeared as waves on the laptop that Lionel was monitoring. Holly pictured the electrical signals racing through the wires, connecting her to Reggie and Lionel like they were three points on a circuit.

Abigail, the girl who had sat next to Holly in Ms. Wilkins's class, had done her sixth-grade science report on electrical circuits. She'd even made a circuit of her own. Holly remembered Abigail's presentation—and all the questions that Holly had wanted to ask but hadn't.

She pushed the memory away and listened closer to the music, her hands hovering over the mixer dials. She felt like she was blundering around in the dark, but it gradually became more instinctual: a slight twist to one dial, then another, to bring the highs and lows of the song into balance. She wasn't sure she was doing it right, but she was doing *something*, at least.

When Reggie finished playing the mandolin, Lionel stopped the recording and Holly lowered her headphones.

"How'd that feel?" Reggie asked.

"Fun!" said Lionel.

"Um . . . fine?" said Holly.

"Fine is a start," said Reggie. "You'll get the hang of it."

He showed Lionel how to create a new track on the recording software that would overlay the mandolin. Then, when Reggie began recording with a fiddle, Holly could hear the mandolin beneath it. It was like Reggie was accompanying himself: two Reggies from two moments in time, coming together in a duet.

After the fiddle it was time for bass guitar, and keyboard, and saxophone. Sometimes Reggie did multiple takes with the same instrument to get one that he liked. The song grew, layer by layer, until it sounded like the work of a full band. Holly was mesmerized by the recording process and by the song itself. It was sprightly but sad, earthy but brassy—and worlds apart from the pop music her dad always played.

Holly lost track of time. When Reggie put down the last instrument and said, "I think that's a wrap for now," she was startled to find that two hours had passed. The pool of sunlight had traveled across Reggie's apartment, illuminating dust motes that hung suspended like spores in the warm air.

"What was all that?" she asked. "I mean, what kind of music is it?"

"Blue jazz!" said Lionel. "Right, Reggie?"

Reggie nodded. "It's a mix of bluegrass music and jazz music."

"Did you invent it?" Holly asked.

"Wish I could take the credit! But no. It's been around for a while. And there are way more skilled blue jazz players out there. But it's rare enough that when I roll into a new town, lots of folks have never heard of it. So I get to feel pretty special. And feeling special is nice sometimes, isn't it?"

Holly thought about how she'd felt when the Save the Grove Committee had accepted her offer to reach out to Alan Kindale, and how she'd felt just now, operating the dial board for Reggie. "Yes," she said quietly.

Questions sprouted in her mind faster than she could ask them. "Is that what you do? Go from town to town and play shows? And isn't that hard? Moving around all the time, I mean. And . . . not having a home." Her voice shook. She forced herself to pause—and ignored an inquisitive look from Lionel.

Reggie didn't answer right away. He collapsed a mic stand and leaned it against the wall, then unplugged a few wires and coiled them up. The silence made Holly nervous. Had she asked too much?

Just when Holly decided she had to say something—*anything*—to break the silence, Reggie said, "My parents split when I was little. I moved around a lot as a kid. My dad was in a bluegrass band. He toured all over Appalachia and I tagged along sometimes. Guess I got used to the van life at a young age. When I wasn't with my dad, I was with my mom in New York City." He pointed at a box of vinyl records. The record on the top of the stack was by someone named Ella Fitzgerald. "My mom's jazz collection. Well, the part of it that she lets me hold on to. She grew up in Harlem, and she's always been obsessed with the Harlem Renaissance. She used to play those records *all day.* So loud, too. Our downstairs neighbor used to come knocking, telling us to keep it down. Kind of like Miss Maisie now."

Reggie paused but Holly knew he wasn't done. It was like a pause in music, she thought, when everything goes quiet, but you know the song isn't over.

"But yeah," he said, standing at the window and looking out at the town square. "Sometimes it's hard. I guess that's why I decided to stick around Arden. I wanted to feel the ground beneath me for a bit."

Holly considered telling Reggie that her parents were divorced, too, and that she also moved around a lot. She wanted him to know that they had a lot in common even if she wasn't a super-talented blue jazz player like him. She wanted to ask him follow-up questions, too—how he'd felt about his parents' divorce, and if his parents had tried to stay friends like hers had, and if they'd ever remarried, and how he'd felt about *that.* But asking a thousand questions would definitely be uncool, she decided, so she only allowed herself one—the same one she'd asked Annie. "But why Arden? You aren't from here."

"Like I said, places give you feelings. I definitely didn't think I'd stay this long, but a couple months back, your uncle invited me to perform at a Save the Grove rally. I learned more about what the committee is trying to do, and I got hooked. The grove is beautiful, but it's how your uncle and the rest of the committee talk about it, too. It means something to them. They're passionate. I like passionate people. Anyway, after that rally, I started landing gigs at the arts center, and some of the restaurants around town, and . . ." He shrugged. "A lot of things in life are complicated. But sometimes they're simple. I think I just like it here."

"And you're gonna stay in Arden for good now, right?" said Lionel.

Reggie laughed. "One day at a time." He started placing instruments back in their cases, then seemed to reconsider. He turned to Holly. "Are you a musician?"

"I can play the recorder," said Holly, a little guiltily.

Reggie gestured around the room. "Pick an instrument. You too, Lionel."

Lionel claimed the box drum before Holly could even

stand. She approached each instrument slowly, sizing it up, afraid to touch anything. Finally, she settled on the most familiar: a small guitar.

Reggie gave her a crash course in guitar playing—how to hold it, how to strum with her right hand, how to move her left hand over the fretboard and press down strings to form a few chords. She couldn't make the chords sound nearly as smooth as when Reggie played them, but it was still fun. The sound reverberated in the guitar and hummed against her body. Looking at the amber-colored wood, she tried to imagine the tree it had come from. *Playing the guitar is like giving a tree a voice*, she thought.

Lionel didn't wait for instruction. He started banging on the drum like his life depended on it, a wild smile lighting up his face. Soon, Holly was fumbling over a three-chord progression and Lionel was drumming off-beat and Reggie was shaking a tambourine. It all sounded terrible and funny to Holly, and it was only funnier when Miss Maisie pounded on the door of Reggie's apartment and hollered, "I'm trying to sell wigs, not concert tickets!"

Then Reggie and Lionel were laughing—deep belly laughs—and Holly couldn't help laughing, too. For the first time in she couldn't remember how long, she laughed until her sides ached. It was weird, she thought, the way laughter could hurt.

Her phone buzzed. There were several texts waiting for her.

From her mom: Just docked in Nassau. How are you? Are you getting along with your uncle? Are you eating enough?

From her dad: Lysander's cough is getting worse. I don't want to jinx it, but I might just be the star on opening night!

And from an unknown number: This is Susan Morales from Vermont Technical Institute. I'll be in Arden tomorrow with two of my students. Can you meet us in the grove at 10 a.m.?

Holly's heart beat like a box drum as she texted Susan back: Yes.

ELEVEN

The next morning, Holly, Uncle Vincent, and Lionel stood in a clearing in the middle of the grove. The morning air was brisk and clean beneath the trees, but through the gaps in the canopy Holly saw factory smoke drifting across the sky like storm clouds.

After Lionel told Holly and Uncle Vincent all about his dream last night, which involved cyborg dinosaurs, hot-air balloons, and a pie-eating contest, he retrieved a crumpled piece of paper from his pocket and handed it to Holly. It was a drawing of a man covered in leaves. "Leaf Man," he explained. "The superhero I invented. Remember? I knew I had a drawing of him somewhere. I had to search my whole room to find it. What do you think? Do you like it?"

Holly wasn't sure what to say. It was fine, but it wasn't . . .

good, exactly. It annoyed her when people showed her things and she was supposed to say "That's great!" when really the things weren't great. She was glad when Uncle Vincent stepped in. "That's nice, Lionel," he said. "I like all the detail in the leaves. You should take a class at the arts center sometime."

"Thanks, Mr. V!"

"Yes," said Holly. "Nice detail in the leaves." She handed the drawing back to Lionel, who recrumpled it and stuffed it in his pocket.

They waited. Lionel made soufflés on his phone. Uncle Vincent closed his eyes. His face looked peaceful in a way that Holly envied. She remembered something he'd said during the Save the Grove Committee meeting: *It was a visit to the grove during my first trip to Arden that convinced me to move here.*

"What was it about the grove?" Holly asked.

Uncle Vincent opened his eyes. "Hmm?"

"At the meeting the other night, you said it was a visit to the grove that made you want to move to Arden."

"Ah—so you were listening."

"Sound carries upstairs," Holly mumbled.

Her uncle smiled, then looked at the treetops. "The light," he said. "See how the sunlight picks up the green of the canopy? And the trunks seem to absorb it, and shine with it?"

Holly nodded.

"The first time I visited the grove, I knew I wanted to paint it. I also knew it was going to take me a while to get the quality of the light just right. And if I wanted to do a close study of the grove . . ." His smile returned. "Well, I figured I should probably live nearby."

It occurred to Holly then that she didn't know when Uncle Vincent had moved to Arden. She didn't know much about his past at all—only the few things her dad had told her over the years, which wasn't much. She felt weird knowing more about Annie and Reggie than she did about her own uncle. Suddenly she wondered how he became an antiquarian, and if he'd ever been in love, and if his heart ever raced when he was trying to nap. She wondered, too, if he ever felt an ache in the center of his chest like Holly had been feeling ever since she arrived in Arden—like she felt right now.

Then came the sounds of footsteps and chatter, pushing the questions out of her mind. Three people emerged from the trees into the clearing. The oldest was a short woman with bronze skin and sharp features. She wore a cargo vest, and her ponytail was pulled through the back of a baseball cap. "Holly?" the woman said curtly.

Holly raised her hand. A smile passed briefly across the woman's face.

"I'm Susan. This is Pritha and Logan." She nodded to the other two—a dark-skinned young woman with cropped black hair and a backpack, and a tan young man with untidy brown hair, glasses, and a shoulder bag.

"This is my uncle Vincent," said Holly. "He's one of the founding members of the Save the Grove Committee. And that's . . . Well, that's Lionel."

"Her friend," Lionel added.

"Thanks for coming all this way," said Uncle Vincent. "We appreciate it."

"It's not too far," said Susan. "And I was intrigued. I've heard of arden trees but never had the chance to study them." She looked around the grove, murmuring to herself, then turned back to Holly. "All right. Tell me again what's going on with the factory."

With help from Uncle Vincent, Holly explained the situation to Susan and her students. Lionel, meanwhile, drifted away in pursuit of a butterfly. Uncle Vincent's eyes followed Lionel as he spoke quietly about the power the Madisons held over Arden. "Town council doesn't want to take a stand against Arden's biggest employer, especially since the Madisons pour a lot of money into the town in other ways."

"Frustrating but unsurprising," said Susan. "Okay, anything else I should know?"

“I’m worried about the trees,” Holly blurted. “They’re losing leaves like it’s autumn but it’s still summer. That isn’t normal, is it?”

“No,” said Susan. “It’s not.”

Holly exchanged a nervous look with her uncle. Sometimes it was nice to be validated. This wasn’t one of those times.

“All right, Pritha and Logan,” said Susan. “Let’s get to work.”

The two students nodded and began exploring the grove. Pritha moved quickly and took lots of pictures with her phone. Logan moved slowly, studying the trees and writing notes in a journal.

Holly didn’t know what to do with herself. Lionel was still chasing butterflies and Uncle Vincent and Susan Morales were deep in a conversation that Holly couldn’t follow—something dreary about small-town politics. Uncle Vincent’s soft voice blended with Susan’s crisp words, each one like a finger snap.

When Holly couldn’t stand still any longer, she joined Pritha at one of the largest trees nearby. Pritha was extracting something from the tree’s trunk with a cylindrical device.

“What’re you doing?” Holly asked.

Pritha smiled at Holly. She had nice teeth. Holly wondered if Pritha used prescription toothpaste for sensitive gums, too. "Taking a core sample," Pritha said.

Holly looked at the tiny hole Pritha had drilled in the trunk. "Does it hurt the tree?"

"Maybe a little. Think of it like a blood draw. We take the smallest sample we can. Just enough material to test." Pritha held up the slender piece of wood she'd extracted. "See these lines? They're part of the tree's rings. They show us how much the tree has grown over the years. Each ring is a different year of growth. Neat, huh?"

Holly already knew about tree rings, but she didn't tell Pritha because she didn't want to seem like a know-it-all. She studied the sample. "The newer rings are smaller."

"Yep. It looks like this tree's growth has been slowing in recent years."

"But why?"

"Not sure yet. We'll have to test these samples at the lab to learn more."

Stop asking questions, Holly told herself. *Let her work.* But when Pritha moved on to another tree, Holly followed. "How'd you get into all this? Working with trees, I mean."

Pritha drew another core sample and Holly flinched like it was her own skin being punctured. "When I was a kid, I went to India every summer to visit my grandparents. My grandpa was a forester. I decided when I was twelve that this is what I wanted to do, and I never looked back." Pritha inspected the new sample. "Same pattern."

She placed it in a glass tube in her backpack.

"I'm twelve now," said Holly. "And my sixth-grade science report was about tree root systems." Immediately she felt foolish. What was a sixth-grade science report compared to a forestry degree?

Still, Pritha looked impressed. "Nice! You're a forester in training. If you want to talk about roots, though, he's your guy." Pritha nodded at Logan, who was crouching at the base of another tree. She smirked and dropped her voice. "He gets a little hyper-focused, but don't be afraid to interrupt him."

Holly nodded and walked over to Logan. He had tugged a root free of the earth and was gently parsing through the intricate white threads that covered the root tips like spiderwebs. "It's a fungus, isn't it?" Holly said.

Logan didn't respond.

Holly cleared her throat and tried again. "It's a *fungus*, isn't it?"

Logan stirred and squinted at Holly. He spoke softly but quickly. "Yes. Exactly. These threads are part of a fungal network in the soil. They connect the roots of different trees. They act like a middleman, transferring nutrients between the trees and extending the roots' access to underground water supplies. In exchange, the fungi get—"

"—carbon and carbohydrates," said Holly. "I know. I was looking at these roots the other day and thought they might be connected to the bushes and grasses in the grove, too."

Logan looked surprised but pleased by Holly's theory. "Certainly possible. A tree doesn't just form underground connections to trees of the same species. It can connect to its other neighbors, too, through the fungal network." His voice grew more animated. "It's not just nutrients and water that are shared. These bushes and grasses probably rely on the shade that the arden trees provide." He brushed hair out of his eyes and looked around the grove. "In an ecosystem, everything works together."

"Why would a tree share anything?" said Lionel. Holly turned to find him standing behind them. "My fifth-grade teacher said that nature is all about survival of the fittest. Wouldn't a tree grow bigger if it kept everything to itself?"

Logan shook his head. He seemed downright excited now. "Sometimes nature is about competition. But with trees, it's about cooperation. The health of the individual depends on the health of the community. See, trees don't do well in isolation. They need to come together and form ecosystems like this one"—he gestured around the grove—"to create the conditions they all need to thrive."

"But these trees aren't thriving," said Holly. "Are they?"

Logan frowned. "I don't think so. Something doesn't feel right."

Holly's attention caught on the word *feel*. She was

embarrassed by what she was about to ask but she asked it anyway. "Can trees . . . ache? And if they were aching, could they communicate that somehow? With us? Could we feel what they're feeling?"

"Leaf Man can talk to trees," said Lionel. "It's one of his superpowers."

Logan blinked at Lionel, then pointed to the fungal threads in his palm. "These are the threads we can see. But . . . maybe there are different kinds of threads connecting trees to us, too. Invisible threads. We definitely rely on trees for a lot of things. Clean air, food, lumber . . ." He clipped away a root sample.

"This is Abenaki ancestral land," he continued. When Holly looked confused, he said, "The Abenaki are the Indigenous peoples of what's currently called 'Vermont.' They're the rightful caretakers of this land. I'm Mohawk, raised in New York City. I'm interested in Native teachings passed down for generations, the work our Indigenous scientists are doing now, and how it all fits into the larger, global conversation. In fact, I'm writing an essay about . . ." The sentence trailed away like one of Uncle Vincent's. Logan blushed and placed his root sample in a bag. "Lots of scientists would probably say trees don't ache. But . . ." He shrugged. "I think there are different ways of knowing."

When Logan moved on and Lionel wandered off, Holly placed a palm against the tree whose root Logan had clipped. The silver bark was cool against her skin. She wished that her touch could somehow stop the leaves from falling. She wished, too, that she could turn back time and see the entire forest that had existed before the factory was built.

Then she heard Pritha and Logan reporting back to Susan. She rejoined the group and waved her uncle over. "When will you know more?" she asked.

"We'll run tests on the core and root samples in our lab," said Susan. "We should have results early next week. Pritha, Logan—I think this could be an interesting summer research project for you both, if it's something you want to keep exploring."

"I'd like that," said Logan.

"Me too," said Pritha. "But if we're going to study this grove, we need it to not be cut down."

Susan nodded. "Vincent, can you put me in touch with a town councilmember? I'll throw my weight around. Let's see if they'll delay decisions on the future of the grove until we have more information. I want to see how prevalent arden trees are in the surrounding area, as well. We need to know exactly how rare these trees are."

"Of course," said Uncle Vincent. "We really appreciate your help. And if there's anything else we can tell you . . ."

"We have everything we need for now."

For the first time that morning, Holly felt relief.

Susan—with her sharp eyes and finger-snap words—was on their side.

Then Holly's phone rang. She stepped aside to answer it.

"Holly! How's Vermont? Tell me everything."

Holly winced and turned down the volume. Her dad's voice was a barreling freight train. The grove didn't seem like the place for barreling freight trains. "Things are . . . still okay. I guess."

"You're a trouper. I'm proud of you, especially because I know you weren't wild about the whole Vermont idea in the first place. And I know Vinny isn't the life of the party, either. So this should come as a nice surprise. Drumroll, please!" Holly did not drumroll. Her dad continued anyway. "I've been thinking maybe we should go home."

Holly's stomach dropped. She took a few more steps away from Uncle Vincent and the foresters. "What are you talking about? What about your play?"

"I just don't know about this one, Holly. It looks like the guy playing Lysander isn't actually sick, so he'll be performing at opening night after all. And that leaves me as Woodland Sprite Number Four. I hardly have any lines. I mean, what am I *doing* here, really?"

"But you *knew* that you'd be playing Woodland Sprite Number Four," Holly said, trying to keep the bite out of her voice. "And just because you can't step in for Lysander on opening night doesn't mean you won't get to step in at all."

"I know. But it's not just the play. San Francisco . . . It's kind of dreary, Holly. Like, the sun is out, but it's never really *warm*."

Holly squeezed her eyes shut. It was happening again. Her dad was falling out of heaven. Usually, this was okay. It meant the end to an adventure Holly hadn't signed up for. But this time it was different. *We should have results early next week*. That's what Susan had said. And it came to Holly like a Fundamental Truth, solid and undeniable: she couldn't leave Arden before learning what was wrong with the grove.

When Holly spoke again, she hardly recognized her own voice—sweet and airy, without a trace of bite. "Maybe you need to give the city and the play a little more time."

"Huh. You think so?"

Holly bit her lip. Was she lying to her dad if she only encouraged him to stay in San Francisco so that she could stay in Arden a little longer? Was she being selfish? And . . . was it wrong to be selfish every once in a while?

"I think sometimes you . . . I think sometimes *people* give up on things too soon. Maybe it's good to give something more of a chance." As she said it, Holly wondered if it was true. The idea frightened her.

"Well . . . there *are* a few more things I want to see around town. And I have a date this weekend." Her dad paused. "It's funny, I thought you'd be itching to go home.

You sure you're doing okay at Vinny's?"

Holly turned in a slow circle. Through the silvery trees, she spied Lionel cupping a frog in his hands. She saw Susan, Pritha, and Logan leaving the grove. And she saw Uncle Vincent standing in the clearing, waiting for her.

"Yeah. I'm okay." Admitting it made her nervous. Okay-ness was a shy, slippery thing. She worried that by acknowledging it, she might scare it away.

"Well . . . good. That's good." Her dad's voice was suddenly gruff, like there was something caught in his throat. "Hey, Holly?"

"Yeah?"

"I miss you."

"Oh. Um. You too, Dad."

Click.

She lingered for a minute after the call, still pressing the phone to her ear. Her heart felt stormy. She *did* miss her dad. She missed all the things about him that usually annoyed her—his big, goofy laugh, and the way his face lit up when he hatched a new scheme. But the time apart was also kind of . . . nice. And it felt strange, missing someone she wasn't quite ready to see again.

She rejoined Uncle Vincent and Lionel. Her uncle told her that he had to go open his shop for the day and invited her along, but she decided to stay in the grove a little longer. Lionel stayed, too. He set the frog down gently in a patch of tall grass, then asked Holly if she wanted to play catch with his bouncy ball. Holly declined.

"Okay, so . . . what now, boss?"

Holly's eyes traced the roots of the arden trees. Several roots seemed to intersect exactly where she stood. She wasn't sure where the idea came from, only that it was what she needed to do, and that it was urgent. "I'm going back to my uncle's house," she said. "I'm going to unpack."

It took a while to find just the right place for everything. Which shirts should be hung in the wardrobe and which should be folded and placed in a drawer? Where should her socks go? And her summer reading books—at first, she stacked them on the window ledge; then, on second thought, she moved them to the bedside table. She knew it was only their temporary home. Very temporary, if her dad couldn't last much longer as a woodland sprite. Still, it seemed to matter.

Eventually, after much deliberation, everything was put away and her suitcase was empty. She slid it under the bed, then assessed her work. The tiny room felt bigger, oddly. Holly thought it should look smaller now that it was filled with her things.

That evening, when Uncle Vincent came upstairs to let her know it was frozen dinner time, his eyes widened. He looked at the quilt she'd laid over the bed (her mom had made it for her years ago) and the picture she'd set on top of the wardrobe (her and her dad on a roller coaster). He smiled, then inspected the vase of flowers on the desk.

"They're wilting," he said. "I can pick up fresh flowers tomorrow, if you'd like."

Holly shrugged. "Up to you," she said. But she hoped he would.

TWELVE

The next morning Holly woke to a knock on her bedroom door. "Sorry," said Uncle Vincent, poking his head in and holding out his phone. "A call for you."

Holly sat up and rubbed her eyes. She was surprised to see her quilt on the bed and her books on the nightstand. It took her a moment to remember unpacking.

She grabbed her uncle's phone, wondering who could be trying to reach her. She'd given her own number to Susan Morales—and besides, as eager as Holly was to hear from Susan, it was too soon for updates. It had only been a day, and it was the weekend now.

Before Holly said a word into the phone, a voice as old as time crackled in her ear. "I heard you've been giving everyone else a hand. Well, today I need help."

"Hi, Beatrice. Um, what do you need help with?"

"Meet me at 235 Marigold Street—and don't dally."

Holly found the small, stout house halfway down the hill from Uncle Vincent's. It took Beatrice so long to answer the door that Holly wondered if she'd gotten the address wrong, but the house's color—a warm yellow gold that reminded Holly of honey mustard—felt just right. At last, the door creaked open and there was Beatrice, in khaki pants and a cardigan and her auburn wig. She peered at Holly through her ginormous glasses and grunted, then ushered Holly inside.

The house was dim—the curtains were drawn to keep out the sun—and the air smelled faintly of menthol. Henry the tortoise was napping on a fuzzy rug in front of a TV that was turned to the news. The volume was low and closed captions were on.

"It took you ages," said Beatrice. "Look at the day, slipping away. It's nearly nine o'clock!"

Holly imagined her protest: *Actually, nine o'clock isn't late at all. Especially on a Saturday. And you woke me, just so you know.* But when Holly met Beatrice's steely gaze, the words died in her throat.

Beatrice pointed a trembling finger at a chair in front of a typewriter. "I have the shakes today, so I need a transcriber for my next *Gazette* opinion piece. Sit."

Holly hated being told what to do. Still, she sat. There was a bouquet of fresh flowers lying on the desk next to the typewriter. Their fragrance almost overpowered the menthol. Almost.

"You *have* used a typewriter before, haven't you?"

"I've never seen a typewriter before," Holly admitted.

With a harrumph, Beatrice showed Holly how to align a sheet of paper in the typewriter. Then she sat on the couch, cleared her throat, and closed her eyes. "'In Defense of the Grove,' by Beatrice Quill."

The typewriter keys felt strange beneath Holly's fingers, and she was surprised by the loud clacking sound they made. When she'd finished the title, Beatrice continued: "I may not be from Arden originally, but I've lived here for fifteen years. That's long enough to know how a town ticks—and where to find its center of gravity. Dear readers, the beating heart of this town is the grove. . . ."

They went on this way for a while, Beatrice dictating and Holly typing and Henry napping. Holly's stomach grumbled. She'd forgotten breakfast in her rush to get to Beatrice's, but she didn't dare stop typing. Her fingers fumbled across the keys and the spelling errors stacked up. She hoped Beatrice wouldn't study the paper too closely.

Three pages later, Beatrice's latest piece was ready to go. "Now to the *Gazette* office," said the old woman. She picked up the bouquet and handed it to Holly. "Carry this.

Henry, that's enough napping. We mustn't be idle."

A few minutes later, Holly found herself walking downtown with Beatrice and Henry. It was an especially hot summer morning. Sweat trickled down Holly's face and her head was thick with hunger and confusion. She didn't know why she was holding flowers. She didn't know why her assistance was still needed. She didn't know when she would be able to eat breakfast—or lunch, at this rate. But each time she almost asked any of these questions, one look at Beatrice's sour-pickle face convinced her to keep her lips sealed.

The town square was only a few blocks downhill, but the journey took ages with Henry. It was remarkably difficult to walk as slow as a tortoise, Holly learned. She kept getting several steps ahead, then pausing while Beatrice and Henry caught up. When they passed people on the sidewalk—"Don't crowd Henry!" Beatrice croaked—Holly wondered if everyone in Arden thought Beatrice was weird for walking Henry on a leash. But then, everyone in Arden was probably used to it by now.

Still. *Holly* thought it was weird. She wished Beatrice had sent her to deliver the opinion piece alone. Then she wished that Lionel was with them. That wish surprised her.

Finally, they arrived at the *Gazette* office. Holly recognized it—she had taped a town hall meeting flyer on the outside wall during Lionel's not-so-official tour of Arden. She held open the door for Beatrice and Henry, then followed them inside, still clutching the bouquet.

It was a messy but cozy office. Desks were strewn with notebooks and photographs and coffee mugs. Since it was the weekend, it was mostly empty, but there was a bald man in a button-up shirt sitting behind a laptop at one of the desks. When he saw Beatrice, his expression wobbled between fear and fatigue.

Beatrice handed her article to him. "This needs to be printed in next week's paper."

"But the deadline for op-eds was yesterday."

"No buts about it! The town needs to read this before the town hall meeting on Thursday evening."

The man looked like he was about to argue, then sighed instead. He scanned the article. "Okay, Beatrice. We'll slot it in. And we'll clean up these typos."

Beatrice pursed her lips at Holly, then turned on her heel and shuffled out of the office, followed by Henry. As Holly followed them, she felt like she had unwittingly become part of a small, strange parade. "Was I supposed to do something with these flowers?"

Beatrice didn't answer. She just kept walking across the square, commanding dogwalkers and joggers and weekend shoppers to make way for Henry. Holly, flustered but intrigued, followed the old woman. Beatrice wasn't walking home. She was turning down a different street, heading to a part of town Holly hadn't been to yet.

It was another impossibly slow journey, only made slower when Henry paused to munch on a cabbage patch by the sidewalk. Holly watched him with envy as her stomach growled.

The street ended at a small graveyard on the edge of town. Worn gray tombstones were scattered beneath the shade of sprawling oak trees. The fence that surrounded the graveyard had nearly been overtaken by ivy. Holly paused at the gate and looked down at the bouquet in her hands. It felt heavy now.

Holly had been to a cemetery before to visit the graves of her grandparents—once after each of their funerals, and a few times later—but she'd never lingered. She was always with her dad, and he was spooked by cemeteries. But Beatrice didn't seem spooked. She walked slowly but purposefully along an overgrown path like it was just another sidewalk, Henry plodding along in her wake.

Holly steadied herself and followed them. She glanced at the family names on the tombs they passed: Watson. Fowler. Smith. Some stones were bigger and fancier than others, with designs engraved in the stone. Holly wondered if those families had more money.

Then they passed the biggest and fanciest grave of them all—an entire mausoleum, as big as Holly's room at

Uncle Vincent's. Holly guessed the name before she saw it carved in the stonework in all-capital letters: MADISON. *Of course*, she thought.

She joined Beatrice and Henry at a modest headstone beneath one of the oaks. Holly looked from the wilting flowers on the grave to the inscription in the stone:

HENRY QUILL

1948–2021

HUSBAND, CITIZEN, REPTILE ENTHUSIAST

Holly studied Beatrice's face. It was pinched and unknowable. The growing silence made Holly anxious, but breaking it didn't feel right, either, and she didn't know what to say. So she stood, and waited, and pressed her hand into her grumbling stomach. The sun beat down. Sweat stung Holly's eyes. Henry fell asleep.

Then Beatrice said, "I wasn't sure about Arden at first. It felt too sleepy, even for retirement. But for Henry, it was love at first sight. He always felt too crowded in Philadelphia, where we used to live. But here, he said he could breathe. He especially loved the grove. A little bit of wild, he called it. Not a landscaped park, but a slice of real, untamed nature. It's a rare thing these days."

"You named the turtle after him," said Holly.

"Tortoise," Beatrice snapped. "In Philadelphia, Henry

volunteered with a reptile rehabilitation center. He loved the tortoises the best. He often asked me if he could bring one home—one of the injured tortoises who couldn't safely be released back into the wild. And I said no, Henry, you most certainly cannot. I was never one for animals—stinky things, always soiling themselves. Well, Henry never made it an argument. He was afraid of arguing. A timid thing, he was. He would just wait a few weeks and ask again, but my answer stayed the same."

Holly looked at the tortoise. "So what changed?"

Beatrice removed the withered flowers from the grave with shaking hands. "Everything," she said. She nodded at Holly.

"You want me to . . . ?"

Beatrice pressed her lips together into a thin line.

Holly placed the fresh bouquet into the vase attached to the headstone, then stepped back as Beatrice inspected her work. Beatrice pushed the flowers down a little deeper into the vase, so it looked like they had sprouted from the earth and grew right up through the stone. Then she said, "You can go now."

"Do you want me to go?"

Beatrice didn't answer. Holly didn't go. They stood in silence while Henry stirred and ate some grass. For the first time, Holly noticed the thin crack running through Henry's shell. Beatrice's words returned to her: *One of the injured tortoises who couldn't safely be released back into the wild.* Again, Holly imagined holding Beatrice's hand, but she didn't dare. Instead, she crouched and gently patted the tortoise.

"It's going to be a fight to save that grove," said Beatrice. "Are you ready for a fight?"

Holly looked up at Beatrice—at the steel in her eyes, and her old skin, lined but tough like tree bark. She imagined her own skin growing thicker and stronger. She imagined she was one of the oaks in the graveyard, sturdy and unmovable, every root an anchor tethering her to the earth. She imagined bending in the wind but never, ever breaking.

"I think so," said Holly. Then, a few moments later: "Yes."

THIRTEEN

Holly kept busy the next week as she waited for Thursday's town hall meeting.

While Uncle Vincent worked at the antiquarian shop, Lionel gave Holly more walking tours of Arden. It surprised her how much there was to discover in a small town. There was maple ice cream to eat, tire swings to swing on, and horses to befriend at a local barn. Holly and Lionel buried their noses in flowers in the community garden, then dared each other to enter an abandoned house covered in vines on the edge of town. When they finally entered the house, they found it bright and breezy inside, with baby sparrows nesting in the rafters.

Day by day, Arden unfurled in Holly's mind. Local faces became familiar. There were the two men who operated a taco truck on Cornelia Street and gave Holly and Lionel free tortilla chips. There was the woman who repaired cars at Arden Auto Shop and blared 1970s rock 'n' roll from a boom box. There was the group of younger kids who played tag in the town square each morning, and their parents, sitting on wooden benches with the latest *Gazette.* Holly came to know the quiet streets, too—how they twisted and turned, where they met and where they branched—until she didn't need her uncle's map anymore.

The only place Lionel didn't take her was the manor house on the hill. Still, they could see the manor from everywhere they went. It was the highest point in Arden, and it stuck out like a sore thumb, boxy and white in a town of kaleidoscopic color.

"That's where the Madisons live, right?" Holly said one afternoon, pointing at the manor from her perch in a maple tree she'd climbed with Lionel.

"Yeah," said Lionel. "Hey, wanna see a funny mural about the year Arden was invaded by, like, a million pigeons? Come on!"

When they grew tired from traipsing through town in the summer sun, they cooled off in Uncle Vincent's store or Annie's Market. They competed to see who could find the oldest book in the bookshop, and who could eat the most scones in under one minute. (Holly won the book contest and Lionel won the scone contest.) They checked in on

Reggie, too, who was editing the song he'd recorded for the grove, and Beatrice, who was already developing her next opinion piece for the *Gazette*: Why tortoises should have the right of way at traffic lights.

Holly wasn't used to her days being so busy or so full of people. But she knew that if she sat alone at her uncle's house while he was at work, she would just be anxiously waiting for updates from Susan Morales on the tree samples that Pritha and Logan had taken from the grove. Between adventures with Lionel, Holly checked her phone, but she only found messages from her parents.

Her dad was in brighter spirits. Lysander's cough had returned, and her dad had enjoyed his first date with a woman named Sylvia. *There's something special about her, Holly. I can feel it!* Holly didn't give much weight to this—he'd said similar things about lots of women over the years—but she was relieved that he seemed happy to stay in San Francisco for a little longer.

Holly's mom, meanwhile, reached out with an unexpected offer. *Our cruise ends next week. You can come stay with us if you need a change of scenery!*

Holly declined. It wasn't that staying with her stepfamily was terrible, but . . . every night in Arden, Holly went to bed excited to find out what Lionel had in store for her the next day. Every morning, she woke up craving Annie's maple scones. She was even beginning to enjoy tea in lieu of coffee, though she'd never tell her uncle.

She knew it wouldn't last, of course. Nothing lasts. But in quiet moments, the realization washed over her, surprising her each time: she didn't want to leave Arden.

She'd never felt this way before—not in Winter Park, or Houston, or Boston, or any of the places she'd lived in or visited with her dad. Even when she enjoyed exploring a new place, leaving always felt natural. Necessary. But now . . .

She reckoned it was just because she had unfinished business in Arden. She had to stay until she heard back from Susan—until the town hall meeting, too. After all, she'd helped the Save the Grove Committee plan for the meeting. And she might even need to stay a little longer after that. The committee was relying on her tree expertise, weren't they? Yes—she was *obliged* to stay. At least, that's what she told herself each time she reached a hand into her pocket to hold the Save the Grove pin that Uncle Vincent had given her.

On Wednesday night—the night before Thursday's town hall meeting—Holly found herself toying with the pin again and staring at her phone. *Early next week.* That was when Susan had said they'd have lab results. But early-in-the-week had already turned into middle-of-the-week and Holly hadn't heard anything.

"Argh!" she exclaimed, dropping her phone on the dining table.

Uncle Vincent stepped out of the kitchen, sweat on his brow and a giant spoon in his hand. "Everything okay?"

"Yeah," said Holly. "Sorry. Um, everything okay with *you*?"

Uncle Vincent smiled uncertainly. "I know you must be sick of frozen dinners, so I thought I'd try making something from scratch. I don't cook much, but Annie gave me this recipe for rainbow pasta salad, and . . . It can't be *that* hard, can it?"

"Do you need help? I make pasta all the time for me and Dad."

"No, no—you've been helping people all week! I can manage this."

And he did. He nicked his finger twice while dicing vegetables and spilled red wine vinegar down his shirt, but finally he set two bowls of rainbow pasta salad on the dining room table. He had a funny expression on his face, somewhere between pride and shame.

Holly inspected her bowl. A fork test suggested that the bowtie pasta wasn't quite fully cooked, and it was still hot, which was all wrong for pasta salad. But she decided to be a good sport about it. "It's very . . . colorful," she said, then put a forkful in her mouth. Before she began to chew, though, her uncle screamed, "WAIT!"

Holly froze with a mouthful of rainbow pasta salad.

"Oh, gosh," said Uncle Vincent. "Holly, I'm sorry. I just

realized . . . You don't like olives. And there are chopped olives in here. I got so swept up in trying to follow the recipe exactly, I didn't even realize . . ."

Horror descended upon Holly. There was only one thing to do: spit out the pasta. But instinctually she was already starting to chew. She squeezed her eyes shut and waited with dread for the first briny taste of olive to hit her tongue.

When it finally did, though, it was surprisingly . . . mild. And blended with so many other flavors that she liked: chickpeas, and tomatoes, and peppers.

"You really don't have to eat this," said Uncle Vincent. "There are plenty of frozen dinners in the fridge. . . ."

"No," said Holly. "No, it's okay." And slowly, to her surprise, she realized that she meant it. *Impossible*, she thought. Olive oil was good, but olives were gross. It was one of the Fundamental Truths of Life. But there was no denying it. The pasta tasted all right, olives and all.

This was concerning. With each bite, Holly felt a Fundamental Truth cracking. What did it mean? If olives weren't always and completely horrible, what else might she be wrong about? Was *anything* true?

After dinner, when she usually went up to her room, she lingered at the table.

"Are you still hungry?" her uncle asked. "There's some ice-cream sandwiches in the freezer. . . ."

"No. It's just—" She paused. Why was this so hard? "I was wondering if you wanted to play that board game you bought," she said so fast all the words strung together.

She figured if she was someone who could eat olives, maybe she was someone who could play board games, too. So, with a feeling of surrender—and a fear that all the pillars of her identity were crumbling—she helped Uncle Vincent unwrap the game and lay out the pieces. They took turns reading the rules to each other, and soon they were deep in a medieval kingdom-building adventure, competing to construct castles and roads across a map that took up most of the dining table.

At first, Holly was annoyed by all the rules. But the game slowly grew on her, and she began enjoying it. Especially when she was winning. "Now I will play my Thief in the Night card," she announced, "which allows me to steal three of your lumber and two of your sheep." She was alarmed by the sudden maniacal quality of her voice, but mostly she felt glorious. She was quickly amassing legions of sheep.

While Uncle Vincent pouted and handed over his cards, Holly's phone rang. She looked at the name lighting up the screen. "Susan!"

Uncle Vincent gestured for her to answer. Holly took a deep breath—it was the call she'd been waiting for, but now she was nervous—and pressed the phone to her ear. "Hello?"

"Do you want the good news or the bad news first?" Before Holly could decide, Susan said, "Let's start with the bad news."

Holly considered stepping away and taking the call in private. Instead, she put Susan on speakerphone so Uncle Vincent could hear, too.

"We analyzed the trunk and root samples, and the results confirm what I already suspected. The trees in the grove are dying."

The words hit Holly in the gut. She curled into herself. It felt impossible—how could a grove die?—but inevitable at the same time, like Holly had known it from the moment she'd first stepped foot in the grove.

Across the table, Uncle Vincent's eyebrows knit together as Susan continued: "I believe Pritha showed you the ring pattern in the trunk cores. There's been less growth each year, with a deficiency of nutrients and cell growth in the newest layers. The roots are nutrient-poor, too, and some of the fungal threads that we sampled are dead, which means the connections between the trees are being severed."

"But *why*?" said Holly. "Why is everything dying?"

"We can't say for sure yet. Probably a change in environmental conditions. We'd like to visit again to collect samples of the soil and the creek water. Factory pollution could be playing a role. And without fungal connections, the healthier trees can't support the struggling trees. We often see a domino effect with this kind of degeneration. Take away one thread from an ecosystem and all the others start unraveling."

Holly felt Uncle Vincent's hand on hers, but it wasn't enough to quell the ache in her chest or the anger warming her face. Images flickered through her mind: The factory smoke drifting over the grove. The old *Gazette* article about how previous generations of Madisons had cut down much of the original forest. The Madison name plastered all across town.

"What's the good news?" her uncle asked.

"We've found arden trees scattered throughout forests outside your town," Susan said, "but we haven't found any dense clusters like you have in that grove. It looks like the grove is a unique ecological phenomenon."

"But how is that *good* news if the grove is dying?" Holly asked, fighting to keep her voice steady.

"It means the grove is worth fighting for," Susan said. "And if we can find out what's hurting the trees, we might be able to stop it or reverse it. I just updated your town council and asked them to continue delaying cutting while we investigate further. I'll let you know when I get confirmation from them.

"In the meantime, Logan and Pritha plan on revisiting the grove to take soil and water samples. They'll also take a few seedlings to see if we can grow arden trees here at the institute's greenhouse. When a species is in trouble like this, we need backups, and it'll give us a chance to learn more about the conditions that arden trees need to grow and thrive."

For the first time since she'd picked up her phone, Holly took a full breath. "Okay. So . . . what can I do?" She looked at her uncle. "I mean, what can *we* do?"

"It takes more than science to protect the environment. A constant annoyance for me, but it's true. People have to care. If they don't, our data goes nowhere. You all keep trying to rally the community around the grove."

"We have a town hall meeting tomorrow evening, actually," said Uncle Vincent.

"Good. Make your voices heard. And I'll let you know when Pritha and Logan pick a time to revisit the grove, in case you'd like to join them. It'll probably be the week after next—I'm taking them to a forestry conference next week." A pause. "Listen, I have to go. My daughter is throwing candy at the TV. More soon. Rosalie, STOP!" *Click.*

Holly stared at her phone. In her mind, she replayed the bad news and the good-news-that-really-didn't-seem-that-good. She felt like the grove was hanging by a thread, and if she made any sudden movements, the thread might snap.

When she looked up, she was surprised to find Uncle Vincent holding his cards again. "I believe you were in the process of stealing my sheep," he said.

Holly wanted to tell him that sheep didn't matter anymore. The trees were dying. The town hall meeting was tomorrow. The grove was hanging by a thread. Didn't he see the thread, as slender as a strand of lacy white fungus?

But she didn't know what else to do, and her uncle was waiting for her, so she picked up her cards, too, and stole all his sheep.

FOURTEEN

Holly slept in on Thursday morning after tossing and turning through much of the night. *The trees in the grove are dying.* Susan's words wormed their way through Holly's dreams and were her first thought upon waking. She sat up, heart racing, and was startled to find it was nearly eleven o'clock. The fresh flowers that Uncle Vincent had placed in the vase on her desk seemed to peer at her, inquiring why she was still in bed.

She felt heavy as she descended the creaky stairs, but when she saw the board game still laid out on the dining room table, she smiled. She had won, thanks to her legions of sheep.

Uncle Vincent had already gone to work, so she brewed herself tea and checked her phone. Usually, she had a text from Lionel by this time, telling her where to meet him. Not today. She looked out the windows of the house in case Lionel might be waiting for her in the yard, but there wasn't a Lionel in sight.

What's the plan for today? she texted him. She felt weird sending it. She'd never initiated a hangout with Lionel before. He was always just . . . there.

Cleaning my room, Lionel texted back. My mom says it looks like a tornado hit and I can't go anywhere until I un-tornado it. The message was followed by seven crying-face emojis.

Holly waited for him to ask for her help. She didn't really *want* to help Lionel clean his room, but she felt she could be persuaded, if he begged and she made it clear it was only because she had nothing else to do and she was a very generous person.

But he didn't invite her.

Holly huffed. Uncle Vincent's house seemed to huff, too. Then Holly realized that she had no idea where Lionel lived. How had he managed to show her all around Arden without pointing out his own house? Each day, they met at Uncle Vincent's or the town square before embarking on their adventures. Why didn't they ever meet at Lionel's?

The question nagged at her as she walked to Uncle Vincent's shop past now-familiar houses. She gave each one a suspicious look, wondering if Lionel was inside, un-tornado-ing his room without her. And all the while, Susan's words played in her head on a loop. *The trees in the grove are dying. The trees in the grove are dying. The trees in the grove are dying.*

The sun peeked out from behind fluffy white clouds as Holly turned down Cornelia Street, warming her skin and quieting her mind. She reminded herself that Susan had asked the town council to delay giving the factory a permit to cut down the grove. Maybe the council would listen to her. And maybe the Save the Grove Committee would build a lot of support at the town hall meeting that night, especially with Reggie performing the song he wrote for the grove.

But when Holly found her uncle sitting at the back of his shop with a newspaper spread before him, her unease returned. Uncle Vincent's face was creased and his eyes were pained. "Holly, I was hoping you'd stop by. The thing is . . ."

Holly looked at the newspaper. It was the latest edition of the *Arden Gazette*, fresh off the press. The front-page headline read:

BREAKING NEWS: Dying Grove to Be Cut Down as Factory Expansion Moves Forward

Holly snatched up the paper and read the article so fast she couldn't understand a word of it, then read it again, forcing herself to slow down. The article explained that a team of foresters from Vermont Technical Institute had made an environmental assessment of the grove and discovered that the trees were dying.

The results of the assessment have hastened Charles and Margaret Madison's plans to build an addition to the Madison Plastics Factory. Late on Wednesday night, the town council approved Mr. Madison's request to cut down the grove. Now he just needs to obtain construction permits for the factory expansion. In an exclusive interview, he told the Gazette *that he intends to obtain the permits quickly and begin construction in early July. "I was, of course, disheartened to hear about the condition of the grove," says Mr. Madison. "But fortunately, we have a plan for making use of that land. The Madison Plastics Factory Visitors' Center and Museum will create new jobs and, by securing the factory's legacy, it will also secure the jobs of the many townspeople who already work at the factory. It's a win-win."*

The proposed construction has been a divisive issue for Arden over the last few months, as Gazette *readers are well aware. The local environmentalists known as the Save the Grove Committee are sure to be disappointed by this news, but Mr. Madison has a strategy for appeasing them.*

"There's no denying that those trees are a part of Arden's history. They gave our town its name and were likely part of the appeal for the town's original settlers. We intend to pay tribute to this history by using lumber from the grove in the construction of the visitors' center and museum. Now the grove will live forever—in the walls of our new facility.

"On a different note, I'm pleased to announce that the Madison Plastics Factory will be funding the design and installation of a modern art sculpture for the town square. . . ."

Holly stared at the article. At first there was only a roaring in her head. Then her face burned and her skin prickled. She was mad. So mad. At so many people.

The councilmembers—how could they do this? Susan had asked them to hold off on issuing permits, not speed up!

The *Gazette*—on Saturday they'd tried to tell Beatrice it was too late for an op-ed, but they managed to write and publish this article in the span of a single morning!

And the Madisons. Most of all, she was mad at the Madisons. Not just for what they were doing to the grove, but for lying. *I was, of course, disheartened to hear about the condition of the grove.* But Holly guessed Mr. Madison wasn't disheartened at all. And the idea that using arden lumber would make everyone happy was laughable. When a tree was felled, when its branches were cut and its roots were severed, it wasn't a tree anymore.

"It's discouraging," Uncle Vincent said. "But we can push back. We still have the town hall meeting tonight—"

"What's the point of the town hall meeting now?" Holly snapped, throwing the paper back on the desk.

"It isn't over till it's over. As long as those trees are standing, it's not too late."

Holly wanted to believe him, but two words were flashing in her head like a neon marquee: *Nothing lasts.* Maybe olives were edible, but this truth was unshakable, and she'd been silly to think that trees were an exception. The grove would fade just like everything faded—every home she'd ever had, every school she'd ever attended, every friend she'd ever made.

As quickly as it had risen, the anger drained away. In its place was a hollow feeling, familiar and comforting. *It doesn't matter,* she thought. *I'll be gone before they cut down the grove and I'll probably never come back. I don't belong here. This isn't my problem.*

She felt foolish—for bringing in Susan Morales and her students, which had only made things worse, apparently; for thinking she had any business getting involved with the fight to save the grove. But mostly she felt tired. She wanted to crawl into bed with a book, pull the covers over her head, make her world small and dark until her dad booked her a flight to Florida, or San Francisco, or wherever he decided she should go next.

She turned to leave.

"Where are you going?" Uncle Vincent asked.

"Your house."

"No." The firmness in her uncle's voice stopped her. "I . . . need your help." He looked around his desk until his eyes landed on a box of yellowed papers. "These are old Arden census records. I need you to sort through them and arrange them by year, and . . . place them in plastic." He nodded. "Yes, that's what I need you to do."

Holly narrowed her eyes, testing Uncle Vincent. Waiting for him to back down. And she knew he would. Because he was frightened of her, she decided. He didn't know what to do with her. She was *too much.* He'd probably been feeling that way ever since she'd arrived.

But Uncle Vincent didn't back down. He coughed and he fidgeted, but he didn't drop his eyes. "It would be great if you could lend a hand," he said evenly.

Holly was surprised. Annoyed. Impressed. She walked slowly back to his desk. "Fine."

Uncle Vincent nodded again—more to himself than to her, Holly thought—and stepped into his little office.

Holly resented her uncle for putting her to work. But soon she found it soothing: checking the date on each census record, slipping it into a plastic sleeve, putting it in its proper place in the stack. It was easy. It was methodical.

As she worked, her eyes skimmed the records. Each page held a long list of family names. Occasionally a name caught her eye—a family that had lived in Arden for generations, or a name she'd seen on a tomb in the graveyard. *Madison. Watson. Jones.*

Then there was the census from 1864. The paper was in poor shape, and the handwritten text had largely faded, but there, in faint cursive: *Foster.*

Holly blinked. It wasn't *quite* Foster. The name was incomplete, the middle two letters too faded to decipher. But there was the *f* and the *o*, the *e* and the *r.* Holly traced the letters with her finger, then carried the census into Uncle Vincent's office. "We don't have any family in Arden, do we?"

Uncle Vincent blinked. "No, no family."

"But . . . did we ever?" She handed him the record. "This is from 1864. The name is faded, but it looks like Foster. Doesn't it?"

Uncle Vincent squinted at the census. "Huh. It's possible, I suppose, but unlikely. I've done genealogical research and have never traced any family lines to Arden, or to Vermont, for that matter. It could be a different name, or an unrelated family with the same name."

"Right," said Holly. "Never mind."

Still, she lingered on the threshold of his office. She thought about Annie opening a market in the same town where her grandmother had taught her to roll dough. She thought about the Madison mausoleum in the graveyard. She thought about her family tree project in fifth grade, and how lots of her classmates came from families that had lived in the same city for generations. It had been so much easier for them to make their trees.

"You said part of the work of being an antiquarian is restoring old documents," she said. "Could you restore this one? Could you bring the full name back?"

Uncle Vincent studied the census closely, turning it this way and that. "I don't know if I could make it more legible, but . . . I can certainly try." Then he looked at Holly the same way he'd looked at the census—like he was holding her up to the light so he could peer inside her mind.

Holly wanted to tell him to hurry. She wasn't sure why, but suddenly restoring the census felt important. It felt *urgent.* Because . . . Well, if Holly had ancestors from Arden, maybe she *did* belong. Maybe she'd always belonged, and her trip to Arden wasn't another random decision by her parents, it was destiny. Maybe every move, and every displacement, and every adventure with her dad had been leading her to this moment—right here, right now, holding her own roots in her hands.

And if she belonged in Arden, then the grove *was* her problem. It was something she could care about. Something she could fight for.

But she was embarrassed by the idea, by the hope, by the way Uncle Vincent was looking at her. So, as casually as she could, she said, "Cool."

Still, the hope was there—a glimmering thing, warm like sunlight and fluttery like the butterflies Lionel chased in the grove.

She returned to the desk but couldn't focus on sorting census records anymore. Her thoughts felt like scrambled eggs. Again and again, her eyes were drawn to the *Gazette*—to the screaming headline on the front page, then to a corner of a page peeking out from the back of the paper.

She tugged out the page and found Beatrice's latest opinion piece, the one Holly had typed up. It was in teeny-tiny font, wedged between ads and classifieds, but it was there, a small but mighty protest. She remembered typing each word. *In a world flattened by concrete, is it too much to ask to spare a little patch of wilderness?* She remembered, too, what Beatrice had told her at the cemetery—*It's going to be a fight to save that grove. Are you ready for a fight?*—and what Susan Morales had said on the phone: *It takes more than science to protect the environment. You all keep trying to rally the community around the grove.*

Then another memory surfaced. Holly flipped through the stack of old *Gazette*s that she'd set aside with Lionel and Uncle Vincent until she found the paper from June of 1924.

Inaugural Arden Midsummer Festival to Take Place this Weekend

Arden is flush with anticipation of the fast-approaching Midsummer festival. Volunteers from the Arden Theatrical Society are busy transforming the grove into a fairyland of lights, while the local orchestra practices new musical numbers day and night. And if the air smells more fragrant than usual, it's no wonder: all across town, citizens are preparing delectable dishes for the festival buffet.

Mayor Arlene Turner says the festival is an opportunity for the town to unite in a special place. "The Arden forest has long drawn people to our humble corner of Vermont. On any day, it is common to see families picnicking, children racing, and people enjoying quiet moments beneath the silver trees. This weekend, we will come together to celebrate what the grove and our community mean to us all. Children can expect to find games and merriment, while adults can savor lively entertainment, libations, and good cheer. . . ."

The article went on to provide a schedule for the festival, including music and dance performances and a tree-climbing competition.

When Holly finished the article, she read it again and again until her brain unscrambled and a single thought crystallized.

She marched back into her uncle's office.

"Uncle Vincent?"

"Hmm?"

"I have an idea."

FIFTEEN

At sunset, Holly and Uncle Vincent walked to the Madison Arts Center, the site of the town hall meeting. A few people who Holly had seen around town were chatting on the building's front steps. She wondered if all the other townspeople were already inside.

As Holly and her uncle approached the entrance, a small person wearing a mask of leaves jumped out of a hedge. Holly screamed and clutched her uncle's arm, drawing the attention of the people on the steps.

"It's okay!" said a very Lionel sort of voice. The leaf monster lifted up the mask for a moment so only Holly and Uncle Vincent could see his true identity. It was, indeed, Lionel.

Holly let her bushy hair fall in front of her face and

avoided the eyes of everyone who had heard her scream. "Why were you in a hedge? And what are you wearing?"

"My Leaf Man mask. I made it last year in my school's art class."

"But *why* are you wearing it?"

"I found it today when I was cleaning my room. It looks cool, doesn't it?"

"It looks *weird*."

Leaf Man looked sad. Holly wasn't sure how, because she couldn't see Lionel's face. Maybe it was the way his shoulders drooped.

"But . . . kind of cool, I guess," she added.

Leaf Man perked up.

"You sure you're up for this, Lionel?" said Uncle Vincent.

"Yeah, Mr. V. One thousand percent. Maybe even two thousand percent."

Holly didn't know why Uncle Vincent was asking. Why wouldn't Lionel be up for a town hall meeting? But as they entered the arts center, a rush of jitters pushed the thought out of her mind. Before today, she'd been nervous about how the meeting would go for the Save the Grove Committee members. Now, after hatching a plan in the afternoon with help from her uncle, she wondered how the meeting would go for *her*.

The center's front doors opened into a small atrium.

There was a framed photograph of the center's grand opening on the wall. In it, Mr. Madison was wielding giant scissors and cutting a ribbon in front of the center. There was a plaque below the photograph: *Thanks to a generous grant from the Madison Plastics Factory, the Madison Arts Center opened to the public in the spring of 2018. . . .*

Holly brooded, but then she thought of the carved wooden figures on her uncle's dining table and the paintings on his walls. He loved the arts center. Holly wasn't sure how to feel about it.

She followed Uncle Vincent and Lionel into the center's largest classroom, which was half full of townspeople sitting on stools at paint-splattered tables. At the front of the room, five people sat facing the crowd solemnly like a panel of judges. "Local government workers," Uncle Vincent whispered to Holly. "See the three in the middle? They're on the town council."

Holly made sure to glare at each of the councilmembers in turn as Uncle Vincent ushered her and Lionel to an open table. The councilmembers didn't seem to notice. This was discouraging.

She studied the other faces in the room. There was Reggie, setting up his music equipment along one wall so he could perform his new song. There was Annie, handing out Save the Grove swag bags and steaming plates of lasagna from foil pans. Beatrice sat in the front row with Henry the tortoise by her feet. Nobody had dared sit next to her yet.

Holly recognized a few other people she'd seen around town, too. There was the man who always wore a bowler hat, and there was the couple who handed out religious pamphlets in the town square. The bald journalist from the *Gazette* stood at the back with a tape recorder. Still, a lot of people were missing.

"Where's the rest of Arden?" Holly asked Uncle Vincent. "Everyone must have seen the flyers for this meeting. I put them up all over town!"

Leaf Man nodded. "She did. I was there."

"This is a good turnout," said Uncle Vincent. "At the last town hall meeting, there were only six people who showed up, myself included."

"Six! Doesn't anyone care about what happens to the town?"

"People care," her uncle said softly. "But they're busy, or tired. They're making food for their kids, or collapsing after a long day of work, or . . ."

"I guess," Holly grumbled.

Soon the meeting was underway. Holly had expected it to be all about the grove, but there was a long agenda of items up for discussion that had nothing to do with the grove at all. A man with bushy eyebrows said that his neighbor's trampoline was almost touching his property line. A woman with dark rouge on her cheeks complained that the air-conditioning at the local post office was still broken. "It's *sweltering*." Then there was the man in the bowler hat, who presented the council with a petition to ban the playing of loud music after nine o'clock at night in Arden. "I've collected thirteen signatures." Holly glanced at Reggie, wondering if Miss Maisie, the wig shop owner, was one of the signatures.

"Are town council meetings always like this?" Holly whispered.

"In Arden, they are," her uncle whispered back.

"But everyone is so *grumpy*."

Uncle Vincent smiled. "Grumpiness can be a form of caring." This struck Holly as a very silly idea, but also a nice one.

Still, with each new topic, Holly grew antsier. She watched the clock on the wall. The hour hand had nearly made a full sweep—and the meeting was only supposed to last an hour.

At last, a councilman said, "On to the last item on the agenda: the grove." Murmurs rippled through the room. The councilman cleared his throat. "I'm not sure if this is still a relevant issue, given the decision made by council last night—"

"If I may," said Uncle Vincent, standing. Holly heard the tremble in his voice but saw the determination in his eyes, too. "I read the news in the *Gazette*, and I must respectfully ask the council to reconsider this decision. I had the chance to meet Dr. Morales, the professor from Vermont Technical Institute, and I believe she advised the council to delay any decisions on the grove until she and her students could conduct further research—"

"Is this professor even *from* Arden?" said the man with the bushy eyebrows. "Why should we listen to her?"

"*You* aren't from Arden, Rick," said the woman with the rouge on her cheeks. "You moved here from Montreal last year."

The room quickly erupted into a debate of who was and who wasn't local, and a contest of who could claim the longest lineage in Arden. The bowler-hat man said that his family had lived in Arden for four generations, but an older woman with long white hair said she could trace her bloodline back to Arden's settlers.

"If I could speak for just a moment," said Uncle Vincent. "My fellow Save the Grove Committee members and I wanted to share what the grove means to us. . . ." But his soft voice was lost in the din. The room only settled down when a councilwoman banged her water bottle on the table like a gavel. "It is the feeling of the council," she said, "that the Madisons have the best interests of Arden in mind."

"And where are Mr. and Ms. Madison?" Beatrice

crowed. She pushed her glasses up the bridge of her nose and looked around the room with magnified eyes. "I don't see them here. Too good to mingle with the regular townsfolk, are they?"

Holly saw Uncle Vincent lay a hand on Lionel's shoulder. She guessed it was because Lionel's Leaf Man mask was getting some weird looks, especially from the bowler-hat man.

"Regardless," said the councilwoman, "the Madisons have given a lot to this town over the generations, including the center where we're all—"

"I'm guessing they've given a lot to the council, too," Beatrice interrupted. "How much does a council decision cost these days?"

The room broke out in noise again—accusations flying, defenses mounting, and an impassioned motion to forget about the grove and return to the real issue: the post office's air-conditioning. The councilmembers and the other government workers looked at each other, then at the clock on the wall. With a collective nod, they stood. "And that concludes tonight's meeting," said the councilwoman with the water bottle gavel.

"But you *can't*!" said Annie. "We've barely talked about the grove at all. And Reggie hasn't even played his song yet!"

"We can continue the discussion at next month's meeting," said the councilwoman.

"Next month?" Reggie said. "Is that a joke? The grove might be gone by then."

Holly looked from Reggie to his equipment—a mic, an amp, several instruments and pedals, all set up and ready to go. She was furious that the meeting was being cut off before he could perform his new song. She was furious that people were standing and heading for the exit and leaving their Save the Grove swag bags behind, the ones she'd put together with Lionel. Most of all, she was furious that she'd run out of time to make her own announcement.

But maybe it wasn't too late. She looked at Uncle Vincent.

"Now or never, I think," he whispered. "Are you ready? I can step in, if you'd like. . . ."

"No. I've got it."

Holly clambered on top of the table and stomped her heel until she caught everyone's attention. She was met with irritated faces, curious faces, encouraging faces, and one leaf face.

Her pulse quickened. She got the same feeling as when she'd interrupted the Save the Grove meeting and suggested reaching out to Alan Kindale—like she was at a circus, walking a tightrope. But this time there were a lot more people staring at her. This time it was a long way down.

"There used to be a festival in the grove on Midsummer's Eve each year," she said. "I don't know when it stopped, or why. But this year it's coming back. So you're all invited to the grove on June twenty-third. That's two weeks from Saturday. There will be food, and games, and . . ." She looked at Reggie. He nodded. "A performance from Reggie Summers. Plus some other cool stuff that we haven't decided yet."

"All of this pending an event permit from council, of course," Uncle Vincent added.

The councilmembers looked at each other. "The application for an event permit can be found on the town website," said one councilman matter-of-factly.

In the quiet that followed, Holly heard the man with the bushy eyebrows whisper, "Who *is* that girl?"

"I think that's Vinny's niece," the woman with the long white hair whispered back.

Holly hesitated. She'd already spent time with a few people in the room, of course, and others had surely seen her around town. Still, introducing herself to all of them felt like driving a stake into the ground. If she remained a stranger, she could still escape Arden without most people noticing or caring. But if she told them her name, that was different. She'd have an identity. She'd be *known.*

Then she thought about the Arden census record from 1864 and that tantalizing half name. That possibility of belonging. She knew it was a long shot, and she was still embarrassed by the hope brewing in her heart, but maybe Arden was in her blood. Maybe she had every right to be known.

"I'm Holly," she said. Then, for good measure: "Holly Foster."

SIXTEEN

Uncle Vincent's doorbell rang several times the next evening. When every seat in the living room was taken, more chairs were brought in from the dining room. There were the usual suspects—Annie, Reggie, Beatrice, and the tortoise—but new faces, too. Ms. Dietrich, who worked at the plastics factory. Miss Maisie, the wig emporium owner. And the man with the bowler hat, who was still collecting signatures for his noise ordinance petition.

As they all chatted and drank the chamomile tea that Uncle Vincent had brewed, Holly pulled Annie aside. "Where did those three come from? I thought it would just be the regular Save the Grove Committee tonight."

"I just happened to mention the meeting to everyone who came into the market today. Your announcement at the town hall last night generated some excitement! The *Gazette* even posted a short article about it on their website. It mentions you by name!"

A shiver ran through Holly. She recalled standing on the table at the arts center the night before, announcing her name to the entire room. And now her name was in the *Gazette.* She felt a little famous. Not quite as famous as Reggie Summers, but still. A *little* famous. Which was weird, and unsettling, and kind of exhilarating.

When the room settled, Holly waited for Uncle Vincent to begin the meeting. Instead, he looked to her with an unspoken invitation and a smile. She stood, then hesitated. Something—or someone—was missing. She looked out the window into the darkening yard. Birches swayed in the wind, but there was nobody there.

"Thanks for coming to this emergency Save the Grove meeting," she said in what she hoped was a very authoritative, leader-of-a-meeting voice. "We're here to discuss the upcoming Midsummer festival. The festival has to be held on Midsummer's Eve, which means we have about two weeks to plan it, which . . . isn't a long time."

She set a stack of newspapers on the coffee table. "These are all the old *Gazette*s from Uncle Vincent's shop that mention the festival. It looks like the festival started in the 1920s and took place every year until the 1950s. It was canceled one year because of a storm, and then everyone just . . . forgot." She passed the newspapers around the room. "I thought we could look through these for details about the old festivals. Like what sort of stuff people planned for them, so we can do some of that stuff, too."

Ms. Dietrich put on reading glasses. "Well," she said, "let's hop to it."

Uncle Vincent placed a vinyl album on his record player and dropped the needle. String orchestras blended with the rustle of old paper and the murmur of conversation as everyone got to work, spreading open the *Gazette*s on the coffee table and floor. The air was thick with the scent of chamomile—and a hint of menthol emanating from Beatrice.

"This one has pictures of the festival," said Annie. "Look at all those lights strung between the trees. It's beautiful! Like a Christmas party in the middle of summer."

"The 1935 festival had a live jazz band and swing dancing," said Reggie, tapping out a rhythm on the coffee table with his fingers. "I didn't know this town had any history with jazz."

"The 1952 festival had a costume contest," said Beatrice. "The winner dressed as a pancake. Bah! What silliness!"

"This paper mentions a tree-listening tradition that happened each year at the festival," said Holly. "I don't really get it, but . . . I guess people, like, talked to the trees somehow?"

"It sounds like there were a lot of activities at the old festivals," said Uncle Vincent.

Holly nodded. "We won't be able to bring back everything. We should choose the things that people in town would like the most. The things that would help people remember that the grove is special."

"It's a nice idea, hearkening back to the old festivals," said Miss Maisie. "But we should do something new, too. Something *surprising*. It's like wigs. Sometimes you want a classic"—she nodded at Beatrice's auburn wig—"and sometimes you want something fresh and startling." She adjusted her own wig—silver streaked with purple—while Beatrice muttered something under her breath.

"As long as the festival doesn't run too late into the night," said the man in the bowler hat with a shudder.

"Simple and elegant," said Ms. Dietrich. "That's the ticket. It's about the trees, isn't it? You don't want too much to distract from that."

Holly was a little annoyed by the newcomers. Were they really committed to saving the grove? And why did they have so many opinions?

But mostly she was happy to see Uncle Vincent's house so full. And to have someone who worked at the factory sitting there, helping plan the festival despite the risk to her job. . . . That meant something, Holly thought.

"Maybe we can each take on one task for the festival,"

said Holly. "Like a group project at school. We can divvy up the work." She decided not to mention that she hated group projects and usually ended up doing all the work herself. Even now, the idea of letting others help plan the festival made her nervous. What if they didn't follow through? What if they let her down?

But she knew she couldn't do it all alone, not in two weeks. She also knew there was a chance she'd have to leave Arden before the festival. Her dad's show would run until then—it was timed so the final performance was on Midsummer's Eve, a fitting end for *A Midsummer Night's Dream.* But she couldn't trust her dad to stick it out for two more weeks if he was already considering throwing in the towel. Holly needed a team who could see the festival through whether she was there or not.

"That's a great idea, Holly," said Uncle Vincent. "I can design flyers for the festival that we can hang around town, for starters."

"I can plan the menu," said Annie. "It isn't a festival without a feast!"

Beatrice pulled a carrot out of the pocket of her cardigan and fed it to Henry. "I'll force the *Gazette* to promote the festival with a front-page feature in next week's paper." Everyone stared at her. She rolled her eyes. "I'll *ask* the *Gazette* to promote the festival."

"I'll work on my setlist," said Reggie. "I have to figure

out how to get a power source in the grove, something to plug into. I'll try to learn more about the music at the 1935 festival, too. Maybe I can do some of the same songs."

Soon everyone had a task: Ms. Dietrich volunteered to take care of lighting, Miss Maisie pledged to rally local businesses around the festival, and the man in the bowler hat offered to design a scavenger hunt. "I used to make scavenger hunts in the grove for my kids," he said, then added morosely: "Now they're in college."

By the end of the meeting, Holly was flush with energy. She felt like she could run for miles without getting tired, which was odd, because she hated running. But when everyone left, she realized there was someone she'd forgotten to assign a task to. "What am *I* supposed to do for the festival?" she asked Uncle Vincent.

He chuckled as he tidied the living room. "You're the festival manager. I'll help as much as you'd like, but you get to oversee everything and make sure we stay on schedule."

Holly liked this. It reminded her of when Lionel called her boss. "I want to learn more about that tree-listening tradition, too. It seems important."

"I'm curious about that, as well," said Uncle Vincent.

Holly chewed on her lip while her brain chewed on all the work ahead. "Hey, Uncle Vincent?"

"Hmm?"

"Have you been able to restore that old census yet?"

He looked at her carefully. "Not yet. Sometimes we can make old documents more legible, but sometimes . . . I'll keep working on it."

"I was just wondering. It's not a big deal." She almost believed herself.

As she helped clean up, she saw that there were several leftover maple scones. It made sense, she thought. After all, the committee's biggest maple scone fan hadn't been there. Once the living room was tidy, she went up to her room to check her phone, expecting an explanation from Lionel. She'd told him about the emergency Save the Grove meeting that morning and he'd said he'd be there.

Where were you? she texted. The meeting just ended!

Usually Lionel texted back right away. This time it took him over an hour to reply. Holly was pretending to read a nonfiction book about the Florida Everglades—but really was just being frustrated with Lionel—when her phone buzzed.

Sorry, boss. I wanted to come but I'm still cleaning my room.

Holly growled. How long did it take to clean a room? If he'd just asked for her help, he'd be done by now!

Then Holly wondered if Lionel was telling the truth.

Holly hated being lied to—hated when her school project partners said they were going to help out but didn't, hated when her dad said they were going to settle down somewhere when they were actually just going to move again. People lied too much. It was why Holly made it a habit to never count on anyone. But now she was counting on lots of people, and lots of people were counting on her.

Suddenly her room at Uncle Vincent's felt too small. Arden felt too small. She squeezed her eyes shut and imagined herself on a busy sidewalk in New York City, or inside a circus tent in Chicago, or on a plane high up in the clouds—places where nobody knew her.

When she opened her eyes, though, she was still sitting on her bed in Uncle Vincent's house in a town that knew her name. She still had a festival to plan, and she still had an ache in her chest, and she was still annoyed at Lionel as much as she told herself it didn't matter.

I don't need friends. It was what she'd told Lionel the day they met. It was why she still hadn't responded to Abigail's text. But what if she was wrong, the way she'd been wrong about olives and board games?

Noise drifted up to her room. Uncle Vincent was watching one of his painting tutorials. Holly didn't like sounds she couldn't control, so she tried burrowing into bed and muffling everything with a pillow over her ears. The silence wasn't as comforting as she'd expected.

She sighed, carried her book downstairs, and made two more mugs of tea—one for Uncle Vincent and one for herself. Then she curled up on the couch to read about the

Everglades while Uncle Vincent painted a cabin by a lake. If there was going to be noise, somehow it felt better to be close to it.

They didn't speak, but every time Holly looked up from her book, Uncle Vincent looked up from his painting and smiled. And Holly wasn't sure how it happened, exactly, but in the course of an hour she went from feeling trapped in Arden to not wanting to leave.

She already knew she wanted to stay until the Midsummer festival, but it wasn't just that. For the first time, she imagined what it might be like to *really* stay. Would there be more afternoons helping Annie at the market, recording music with Reggie, or writing opinion pieces with Beatrice? Would there be more evenings like this—reading on the couch while Uncle Vincent painted, breathing in the ginger and turmeric wafting up from steaming mugs?

The words in her book blurred. She knuckled her eyes. *No daydreams*, she told herself.

She tried to focus on the Florida Everglades—those swampy mangroves and cypresses, so different from the trees of the northeast. But as the night wore gently on and her body grew soft and heavy, the daydreams returned and slowly morphed into real dreams.

SEVENTEEN

The next week was a flurry of activity for Holly.

It started with a text from her mom on Sunday morning. Back from the cruise! Can we video chat? I want to see you!

Just a sec, Holly replied. She tidied her room, then propped her phone on the window ledge by her bed. A minute later, her mom's face filled the screen.

"You look great, hon!" her mom said.

Holly didn't know what this meant. Didn't she look the way she always looked? "Thanks," she said. "You look . . . tan."

"I look *burned*," her mom said.

She went on to tell Holly all about the cruise. Holly half listened. Hearing about a trip she hadn't been invited on annoyed her even though none of the activities her mom described sounded like Holly's idea of fun. Tanning on the beach of a resort island? Holly hated sand. A cabaret show at the ship's theater each night? Absolutely not.

"What about *you*?" her mom said, running her fingers through her hair—frizzy, untamable hair, just like Holly's. "How's Arden?"

"Fine," said Holly, because that was what she always said. Her mom pressed for a longer answer, though, so Holly offered a few details. She talked about exploring town—without mentioning Lionel. She talked about maple scones—without mentioning Annie. She worried that if she talked about who she'd been spending time with, well . . . her mom might think she'd made friends. And she was specifically *not* making friends.

She didn't mention the Midsummer festival, either. The idea of her parents knowing that she was so involved with something—that she was putting so much *effort* into something—was embarrassing, somehow. And what if the festival went all wrong? No—best not to bring it up, she thought.

Still, her mom seemed to suspect something. "You seem a little different," she said, squinting at Holly through the camera. "I don't know what it is, but . . . it's *something*."

Holly blushed and told her mom she had to go eat breakfast.

"Yes, eat! Topher just woke up, so it's time for eggs and toast here. But it was good to see you for a minute. Oh—do you have enough toothpaste?"

"Yes," said Holly. "Like, a lot."

"Good! Better safe than sorry. Love you, hon."

"You too, Mom."

For the rest of the week, her mom's words echoed in her head: *You seem a little different.* But Holly shrugged them off and kept busy overseeing the festival preparations and lending a hand wherever she could. One moment she was hanging Uncle Vincent's festival flyers across town, the next she was tortoise-sitting while Beatrice visited the *Gazette* office to demand they promote the festival in their next issue.

When Holly asked why Henry couldn't go to the office, Beatrice said that conflict was stressful for the tortoise—and when Holly asked if she could visit the *Gazette* in Beatrice's stead, Beatrice shook her head. "Those journalists fear me. They'll do what I say." Holly couldn't argue with that, so she watched TV at Beatrice's house while Henry snoozed beside her on the couch, and she wondered if every festival manager had to tortoise-sit at some point.

She paid Annie a visit, too. The kitchen at the back of the market was a culinary crime scene—flour and dough and batter everywhere, strawberry sauce trickling down the counters like blood, and a knot of sweet and savory scents that Holly's nose couldn't untangle.

"So much to do, so little time," said Annie as she whipped through the kitchen at light speed.

"Can I help?" Holly asked.

"Have you ever filled doughnuts with cream?"

"No, but I can learn."

And she did. Annie showed her how to poke small holes in the doughnuts and use a piping bag to fill them with strawberry cream. "Here's a little trick I learned from my grandma," said Annie. "Put a small spoonful of jam on top of each doughnut after you fill it. That way, we know which ones are done. Plus, it's tasty!"

Holly also helped Annie mash bananas for banana bread and dice onions and peppers for savory tarts. "You know you don't have to make *all* the food for the festival," Holly said. "Uncle Vincent's flyer says it'll be a potluck and people should bring food and drinks."

"I know, I know. But what if everyone brings the same thing? What will we do with a hundred bags of tortilla chips?" Annie leaned against the counter and caught her breath. "The thing is . . . my parents really aren't doing well in Burlington. I promised them I'd move there next month. So I just want this festival to be great. It feels like my last hurrah. For now, at least."

Holly tried to imagine Arden without Annie. It was hard. "Have you hired someone to take over the store?"

"Not yet," said Annie. "I'm being too picky, I know. It's just hard to give this place away, even if it's temporary."

"So you do think you'll come back to Arden? Eventually?"

Annie was quiet. She slid a tray of tarts into the oven and cleaned the counter. Just when Holly thought she wasn't going to answer, Annie wiped her hands on her apron and said, "In my heart, all roads lead here."

Holly imagined all the roads of the world twisting and turning and eventually meeting in the tiny town of Arden, like roots all leading back to a small, strange, wonderful tree. And there it was—the ache in her chest.

"Where's Lionel, by the way?" Annie asked. "I thought you two did everything together."

Holly frowned. "Not *everything*," she said. But she didn't have an answer for Annie.

Throughout the week, Lionel drifted in and out of the festival preparations. He helped Holly hang a few flyers, but he looked over his shoulder at every turn, and he scurried home before they were halfway through the stack. He said he was too busy to tortoise-sit or help out at Annie's, and on Friday—eight days before the festival—he acted stranger than ever. Which was really saying something, Holly thought.

That afternoon, Holly and Lionel met Reggie at the grove to help him test out his concert setup. Reggie parked his van outside the factory and carried a small electricity generator into the grove. "This was lying around at the thrift shop downtown. The owners let me rent it for a week for free. They seemed pretty excited about the festival."

Holly flushed with pride—and quivered with nerves. The town was looking forward to the festival. Now she had to make sure it lived up to everyone's expectations. After all, the town would know who to blame if it didn't. *She* was the one who'd announced the return of the festival. It was *her* name in the article about the festival on the *Gazette*'s website. So if the festival was a flop . . .

Her mind conjured frightful images: everyone showing up to the event and saying, "What a *mess*." Or worse—nobody showing up at all. She imagined Uncle Vincent's face turning red with embarrassment. . . . He'd regret ever inviting her to Arden, and she'd leave town in shame. . . .

A sudden rustling in the tall grass snapped her out of it. It also gave Lionel a spook. He darted off and tucked himself into the cavity of a hollowed-out arden tree. A moment later, a squirrel emerged from the tall grass, carrying a nut in its mouth.

Holly tracked Lionel to the tree. He was squeezed tight inside, surrounded by bugs and worms that wriggled across the decaying wood.

"What're you doing?"

"Playing hide-and-seek."

"Who are you hiding from?"

He plucked a beetle off his arm and set it back on the tree. "Um . . . you? You win!"

Holly narrowed her eyes. Lionel was jumpy. He was on edge. But *why*? She nearly asked, but. . . . Asking Lionel what was wrong would mean that she *cared* what was wrong. And caring what was wrong with Lionel seemed dangerously close to being friends with Lionel. *Lionel is my Arden tour guide and my festival planning partner*, she thought. *Not my friend.* It felt good to remind herself of this. Everything made a little more sense, like she was squeezing the whole world into a box and closing the lid and sitting on it.

With that settled in her mind, Holly busied herself helping Reggie run wires from the generator to his music equipment.

"What're those?" she asked, pointing to a few pieces of gear.

"Loop pedals. Here, I'll show you."

Reggie turned on the generator and picked up his mandolin, then stepped on one of the pedals and played into a microphone. "It's like a recording. See?" When he stepped on the pedal again, the mandolin melody he'd just played poured through the speakers on a loop. He accompanied it with a box-drum beat, pressing his foot down on another pedal. "This is how one guy can become a band. Layer by layer."

The music sounded bigger in the grove than it had in Reggie's apartment. Grander. When the trees swayed in the wind, Holly imagined that they were dancing to the song—and that reminded her of the tree-listening tradition she'd seen mentioned in an old *Gazette.*

Once Reggie felt good about his setup, Holly helped him load the equipment back into his van. Lionel lingered on the edge of the grove, watching them from behind the trees like a shy monkey—which was odd, Holly thought, because Lionel definitely wasn't shy.

"You two need a ride anywhere?" Reggie said.

"Just down the street," said Holly. "I'm going to my uncle's shop."

"Lionel? How about you?"

Lionel looked both ways, then ran from the grove and hopped into the van next to Holly. "I'll go to Mr. V's, too."

It was a tight fit—the van was full of boxes, loose clothes, and music equipment. "Sorry," said Reggie, pushing aside a pile of coats to make more room. "I never totally unpacked. When you're used to living out of a van, it's weird to empty it."

As Reggie drove them down Cornelia Street, Holly sifted through a pile of road maps and brochures at her feet. New River Gorge National Park. White Mountain

National Forest. The Washington, DC, subway system. Holly thought about all the places Reggie must've been in his life. Maybe some of them were places she'd visited with her dad. And somehow, she and Reggie had both wound up in Arden working together to save a grove. Holly didn't believe in fate, but her mind turned again to the census record, and she wondered.

Reggie stopped the van outside the Arden Antiquarian Shop. Holly climbed out, then looked back at Lionel. "You coming?"

Lionel stared at the shop. His eyes were wide and shimmering. Then he looked away. "Actually . . . I should probably go home."

"Let me guess. You need to clean your room."

Lionel smiled weakly. "See you later?"

Holly wanted to accuse him of lying. She wanted to demand answers, to shake him by the shoulders and tell him to be normal Lionel again. Roller-skating-into-streetlamps Lionel. Bouncing-a-bouncy-ball and eating-all-the-maple-scones Lionel. She missed that Lionel.

Tour guide and festival planning partner, Holly repeated to herself. *Not my friend. Not my business.*

Still, she lingered on the sidewalk as Reggie drove away, waiting to see where he went to drop off Lionel. Soon, though, the van turned a corner and disappeared from sight.

Holly felt irritable as she entered Uncle Vincent's shop, but she perked up when her phone buzzed with a text from Dr. Morales. Pritha and Logan will revisit the grove on Monday afternoon to take more samples. And she felt even better when her uncle told her that the town council had just approved the event permit for the festival. She was relieved—and a little surprised.

"Councilmembers might rely on the Madisons for funding, but they're elected by the town," Uncle Vincent explained. "And the town is excited about the festival."

Then Holly noticed that Uncle Vincent was working on restoring the census record. "How's it going?" she asked.

"It's hard to say," said Uncle Vincent. He was slowly rubbing a sponge over a corner of the paper.

"The name is down here," Holly said, pointing. "Not up there."

"Restoration is a delicate art. There are several ways to treat old paper, but the treatments can make things worse if you aren't careful. This is a chemical solution. I'm not sure how the paper is going to react, so I'm testing it up here in the corner first."

"But you *have* done this sort of thing before, right?"

"Oh, yes. Lots of people hire me to restore old documents. I have a whole stack waiting for me in my office!"

Holly exhaled. For a while, she watched Uncle Vincent work, but his slow pace was maddening. She wanted to snatch the sponge and give the whole paper a quick rubdown. She imagined uncovering the name *Foster* like it was a secret root buried deep beneath the soil.

Instead, she flipped through the old *Gazette*s that mentioned the Midsummer festival, looking for more information about the tree-listening tradition. Several papers mentioned the tradition but didn't explain it. But then, in a paper from June of 1938, the tradition was given a whole paragraph in an article about that year's festival.

"It says here that there's an old local legend that arden trees can grant wishes," said Holly. "Except, instead of giving you something you *want*, they give you something you *need*."

"Intriguing," said Uncle Vincent. "What if someone isn't sure what they need?"

Holly kept reading. "That's where the tree-listening tradition comes in. At the old festivals, everyone found their own arden tree. They'd stand in front of the tree and close their eyes and the tree would *listen* to them. Not to what they said, but to their heart."

"And what did people give the trees in return?"

"Huh?"

Uncle Vincent ran a soft brush across the census record. "If the trees listen to us, it only seems fair that we listen to them, too."

Holly thought back to something she'd read when she

researched trees for her sixth-grade science report. With highly sensitive microphones and ultrasound equipment, scientists could detect sounds coming from inside thirsty trees—little clicks and fizzles as water columns broke and bubbles formed. She also thought back to something Logan had said. *Maybe there are different kinds of threads connecting trees to us, too. Invisible threads.*

She was glad that Logan and Pritha were returning to the grove on Monday. It felt good to have something to look forward to before the festival. Something else that might help save the grove.

The bell over the shop door jingled. While Uncle Vincent helped a customer find books on farming, Holly peeked at the census record. The name wasn't any more visible. Not yet. Still, she dared to hope that the name would be revealed—and that it would be hers. Then she'd have hard evidence of her connection to Arden, evidence that her roots here ran as deep as those of the Madisons and every other family who had lived in town for generations.

The hope felt foolish. Improbable, even. But she couldn't help it. Because for the first time in her life, Holly had the sneaking feeling that she might belong somewhere.

EIGHTEEN

Holly yawned as she arrived at the grove on Monday afternoon. It had been a long weekend of festival preparations, and the sun was making her drowsy. She was grateful for the arden trees. They stood over her like sentinels, casting shade and cooling the air. The canopy was patchy—leaf loss, Holly guessed—but it still made a soft, green sky.

At first the grove was silent and still, like Holly had walked into one of her uncle's paintings. But then the tall grasses stirred; the creek burbled; bugs crawled out of knots in the bark of arden trunks while robins and thrushes alighted on branches and cocked their heads at Holly. She smiled with the pleasure of being the sole witness to nature's secrets.

She walked toward the small clearing in the heart of the grove, pausing in front of certain trees that caught her eye. She still wasn't totally sure how the tree-listening tradition worked. How did someone decide what tree to stand in front of? There were so many. And how could you know if the tree was really listening? Did it only work on Midsummer's Eve? Not that she actually believed in the legend, of course, but . . . hypothetically.

She found a tree with large roots that spread from either side of the trunk and formed a crescent moon in the soil. Then she stared at the tree's silvery bark and took a deep breath, trying to ignore the voice in her head accusing her of being unscientific.

Um . . . Can you hear me? she thought.

Is it working?

Hello?

There was no obvious response, no treelike voice in her head saying *Yes, I hear you, Holly Foster. How do you do?*

She wondered if she needed to try harder. She planted her feet. She scrunched up her face in concentration until her cheeks ached. She didn't move, not even when a mosquito buzzed around her. Soon she had a headache and an itchy arm but no response from the tree. She was relieved when her phone rang.

"Alaska," her dad said instead of hello. "You and me in Alaska. A week. Maybe two weeks, if we can swing it.

Doesn't that sound amazing?"

Holly winced. She missed her communion with the tree, even if she'd been doing it all wrong. "Wait, what?"

"I've been reading about Alaska all morning. We could have a real adventure. Hiking, canoeing—"

"The last time we hiked, you twisted your ankle."

"—and they have these wild reindeer called caribou."

"Slow down, Dad. Alaska? Where is this coming from? And do we even have the money for that kind of trip?"

"Holly, how many times do I have to tell you? Don't worry about money! That's for *me* to worry about. Now, come on—what do you think? Wouldn't it be fun?"

Holly couldn't see her dad, but she could imagine just how he looked: wide-eyed and smiling big, bouncing on his heels like a kid at a candy store. Holly, meanwhile, got the feeling she always got when her dad suggested a new adventure: mild curiosity mingled with bone-deep fatigue. "I guess. Maybe. But when?"

"We should do it while you're still on summer break! Maybe July. Or . . ."

Holly's grip tightened on her phone.

". . . we *could* go now."

"Now?"

"I know, I know. It's a crazy idea. But I just feel this *energy* around it."

"What about your play?" Holly spluttered. "I thought

you were going to give it a chance!"

"I've *been* giving the play a chance. But it got a . . . not-so-great review in a local paper, and we aren't drawing a huge audience. I think it might be a sinking ship."

"But—but you just had a date with someone in San Francisco, didn't you? Someone you liked?"

"Sylvia," he said. "It's good. She's good. But . . . I don't know. Sylvia and I, we both have a lot going on right now, and I'm not sure she really *gets* me."

Holly pressed her fingers into her aching forehead. She imagined burying her phone in the dirt beneath her feet so she'd never have to have this conversation again. The places, the plays, the women—they changed with the seasons. The conversation didn't.

Except this time it *was* different. Because this time Holly knew exactly where she wanted to be. And it wasn't Alaska.

"The thing is, I'm kind of busy here. In Arden. Right now."

"Oh," said her dad. It was a surprised *oh.* A hurt *oh.* And Holly felt guilty, but she felt angry, too. All her life her dad had decided where she would go, and when, and for how long. When would *she* get to decide?

"Can we talk about this later?" She nearly said *after the Midsummer festival* or *after Uncle Vincent restores the census.* Instead, she said, "After your show ends."

Her dad was quiet. Her dad was rarely quiet.

"And I'll think about Alaska in the meantime," Holly added. "It could be fun."

"Think about it," her dad said. "It could be awesome. But . . . we don't have to decide right now." Holly knew this wasn't an easy thing for her dad to say. For him, *right now* was always a good time to make a big decision.

"Okay," said Holly. She looked down and stirred up soil with the tip of her shoe. "Hey, Dad? I know you don't know much about your ancestors and stuff, but do you know if any Fosters ever lived in Vermont? Before Uncle Vincent, I mean."

"Not that I know of. Why?" Before she answered, her dad went on: "It's funny. Vinny was the one who got into the family history stuff. He used to email me about it. He'd done all this work on a genealogy website, but I could never make head or tail of it."

Holly found herself wishing she'd known Uncle Vincent better back in fifth grade when she'd attempted her family tree project. "Why is that funny?"

The sounds of wind and car horns came through the phone. Her dad was on the move. "Vinny was the one who left the family," he said above the din, "so I was surprised he got into all that."

Holly pressed the phone harder to her ear. "What do you mean he left? Why did he leave?"

"Hey, Holly, can I call you back in a bit? I'm catching a cab."

Holly was about to protest, but then she saw Pritha and Logan walking toward her. "Yeah. Okay."

"Love you, kid."

"Love you, too," said Holly, feeling more tired than when she'd arrived at the grove. She hung up as Logan and Pritha joined her in the clearing.

"Glad to see they haven't cut it all down yet," said Pritha.

"They will as soon as they can," said Holly. "The factory just needs a construction permit."

"Well," said Logan quietly, "let's hope they get bogged down in some local bureaucracy."

Holly didn't know what bureaucracy was, but the idea of the Madisons getting bogged down in anything sounded nice. She pictured Mr. Madison floundering in a Florida swamp, and she only felt a little guilty for it. "Yes," she said. "Let's hope."

Pritha popped in earbuds and listened to music while she worked, but she still explained to Holly everything she was doing without Holly having to ask. "We're taking soil samples from a bunch of spots around the grove. We'll take some creek water, too. We can test the soil and water in the lab and see if they tell us anything about why the trees are sick."

Logan, on the other hand, required nudging. Sometimes

Holly had to repeat a question several times before she caught his attention, but it was worth it. Logan saw the little details—and when Holly listened to him, she saw them, too.

"See how the root network is denser near the creek?" he said. "The roots are drawn to the water. So if there's something wrong with the water—"

"The trees could be poisoned."

"Exactly."

Holly watched Logan collect water samples in glass tubes. It was starting to feel like a mystery. She imagined Pritha and Logan as detectives, snooping through the grove and hunting for clues. She hoped they cracked the case soon.

After collecting samples, Pritha and Logan searched for arden seedlings.

"What're you looking for, exactly?" Holly asked.

"Baby trees," said Pritha. "They'll be small. There are a few over there, see? But they don't look healthy enough. Poor things."

Logan crouched by the drooping seedlings. "Usually, the biggest trees in a forest support the seedlings. They send nutrients through the network of roots and fungi."

"I read about that when I was doing my science report," said Holly.

Logan nodded. "Trees support each other."

"So if the seedlings aren't healthy—" Holly began.

"The fungal network might not be doing its job, or the big trees don't have anything left to give." Logan adjusted his glasses. "We'd expect to see more new growth here after the spring season, too. The lack of seedlings is another sign the grove isn't doing well."

"What about that one?" said Holly, pointing to another tiny arden tree. This one stretched up and out with thin, leafy branches, like it was asking the bigger trees for a hug.

"Bingo," said Pritha. "Nice catch!"

When Pritha and Logan began to uproot the seedling with spades, Holly felt a twinge of regret. "What're you going to do with it?" she asked, resisting the urge to shoo them away and guard the baby tree with her body.

Pritha wiped sweat off her brow. "Replant it in the greenhouse at our school. And it's good timing. We were at a forestry conference with Dr. Morales last week, and there was a seminar on growing seedlings in greenhouses. Now we can put what we learned into practice!" She looked at Holly. "You *have* to see our school's greenhouse sometime. It's really cool."

"In the greenhouse, we can study its growth and learn more about its needs," said Logan as he teased apart the seeding's roots. "We'll take a few seedlings, and if we can raise them and get them to reproduce, we might be able to grow new arden trees that can be replanted elsewhere.

Then we can help the species recover if this grove is cut down or dies."

"But arden trees only grow in this area," said Holly. "That's what my uncle told me."

"Our school's only an hour away," said Pritha. "I bet the climate and soil are similar enough at the college for the trees to grow there."

"But the roots," said Holly as Logan lifted the seedling out of the ground. "You're taking them away from the fungal network. It's like you're . . . unplugging them."

"Last time we were here, you wondered if the arden trees were connected to the bushes and grasses," said Logan. "Remember?"

Holly nodded.

"Trees can plug into fungal networks with plants of different species. Hopefully, the arden trees will tie in to the fungal network that's already growing in the soil of the greenhouse." He looked at Holly. "Trees are sensitive. But they're resilient, too. They find ways to survive. Especially when they aren't alone."

As Pritha and Logan uprooted two more seedlings, Holly felt a jumble of emotions—distress for the trees being taken from their home and their family, but hope, too. Hope that they could take root in the greenhouse at Vermont Technical Institute. Hope that they could find a new home in fresh soil away from the factory and the

Madisons, so that if the grove was cut down, at least there were survivors.

She helped Pritha and Logan carry the seedlings back to Pritha's truck, which was parked outside the factory gates. Holly had taped Uncle Vincent's festival flyers to the gates over the weekend, but they were gone now. She peeked inside a trash can on the sidewalk and found several balled-up flyers buried beneath banana peels and plastic wrappers.

"Ugh!" she exclaimed.

"You okay?" Pritha asked.

Holly plucked out a flyer and smoothed it out, then handed it to Pritha. "I'm fine, it's just—there's a festival in the grove this Saturday. It's based on this historic festival that used to happen in Arden every year. The whole town is invited. You two can come, if you want. Dr. Morales, too. I mean, you all don't *have* to come. I know you're probably busy. But—"

Pritha smirked. "Susan *does* love a good party."

Holly tried to imagine Susan Morales at a party. "Really?"

"It's true," said Logan. "She's always the first one on the dance floor at forestry department holiday parties."

"And *you're* always the last," said Pritha, grinning and poking Logan in the arm.

"There will be music," said Holly, pointing to one of the

bullet points on the flyer: *Featuring the musical stylings of Reggie Summers, local blue jazz sensation.*

"Nice," said Pritha. "We'll pass along the invitation."

"And you'll let me know what you find out when you test the samples?"

"Dr. Morales will give you and your uncle a call when we have results," said Logan.

After Pritha and Logan drove off, Holly stood on the sidewalk, staring at the belching smokestacks of the factory and wondering what to do with herself. Then she retrieved another crumpled flyer from the trash can and tucked it into the metal latticework of the fence that surrounded the factory.

She nodded. "Your move, Madisons."

NINETEEN

On Thursday, two days before Midsummer's Eve, Holly woke early in the morning. She was shaky with anticipation. Time was moving too slow and too fast. She was eager for the festival to arrive but there was still so much to do.

While she brushed her teeth with her prescription toothpaste, she mentally reviewed the festival to-do list. Ms. Dietrich had collected Christmas lights from townspeople, but they still needed to be hung around the grove. Annie was whipping up dishes and treats, but buffet tables still had to be gathered and arranged beneath the trees. Miss Maisie had convinced the owners of several local shops to attend the festival, but they all wanted to set up booths in the grove where they could promote their businesses.

"It's a *lot*," Holly announced while eating breakfast with her uncle.

He cupped his mug of tea with both hands. Steam drifted past his face. "Yes, we're being quite ambitious, aren't we? But you're doing a great job keeping things moving, Holly. And you aren't alone." He looked her in the eye. "You know that, right?"

Holly nodded. He was right. She wasn't alone—which was a strange thing to admit to herself. Uncle Vincent was helping her every step of the way, and the other Save the Grove Committee members were cheering her on, too. Even Beatrice. And Holly appreciated it—but again and again, her thoughts turned to Lionel. She kept trying to enlist him to help her, but now he had a cold and couldn't leave his house. At least, that's what he texted Holly. She still had the nasty feeling he was lying. She was still determined not to care.

After breakfast, Holly and Uncle Vincent walked to the grove and hung the lights that Ms. Dietrich had provided between the trees. Holly felt like they were dressing the trees for a theater show as they looped the lights around silver trunks and strung them from branch to branch. When they plugged the lights into the generator that Reggie had found, Holly's heart fluttered.

"It looks like the festival pictures in the old *Gazettes*," she said. "Doesn't it?"

"It does," said her uncle. "Even brighter, I'd say."

Then Holly noticed that, without trying to, she and her uncle had arranged the lights in a way that mimicked the trees' roots. Almost all the strands of lights originated from three of the largest trees in the grove, then moved outward to smaller trees and saplings. *Like the roots of the parent trees feeding the young ones,* Holly thought.

"How could anyone tear all this down?" she asked.

"Maybe they won't," said Uncle Vincent.

"Maybe they won't," said Holly, because repeating things made them feel truer. "I still don't understand why the factory has to build here. There's plenty of land outside of town."

"We wondered the same thing," her uncle said. "Before you came to visit, the Save the Grove Committee asked the factory to consider building elsewhere. But they argued that the new visitors' center and museum need to be attached to the current factory building. So this is the spot—unless they tore down some of the shops on Cornelia Street."

"They can't do that, either!"

Uncle Vincent gave her a smile—small but more reassuring for its smallness. Holly didn't trust big smiles.

"At least the factory isn't getting in the way of the

festival," Holly said. Ever since she'd stuck the festival flyer back on the factory gates, she'd been expecting some kind of clapback from the Madisons. She wasn't sure what, exactly, but . . . *something*.

"I'll admit I feared they might find a way to shut this down," said Uncle Vincent. "But it's all moving smoothly, and the town council has been supportive." He clasped his hands behind his back and turned in a slow circle, studying the grove. "The festival will remind everyone that Arden is more than a factory town."

"I hope so," said Holly. It wasn't an easy thing to say. Admitting to hope made her nervous. But she suspected that Uncle Vincent felt the same way, and being nervous together was better than being nervous alone.

"Hope," he said, "is a brave thing."

Holly turned the words over in her head as she walked with her uncle down Cornelia Street. He went into his shop to open up for the day, but Holly kept walking. Her uncle was right—it was a lot of work, but the festival preparations *were* going smoothly. And that meant it was time to reward herself with a maple scone.

She wasn't sure if she was imagining it, but she sensed a different energy in downtown Arden as she walked to Annie's Market. Everyone she saw on the sidewalk seemed to move a little lighter and smile a little wider. It was like the air was buzzing with excitement for the festival, and everyone who breathed it in was lit up from the inside.

Holly felt lit up from the inside, too. The ache in her chest hadn't gone away, but there was a warmth there now, too, like her heart was a little sun. The feeling surprised her. Even more surprising, she found herself smiling at everyone she passed.

When her phone rang, she answered brightly: "Hi, Dad. What's up?"

"It's happening," he said. "It's really, actually happening." He paused for dramatic effect, then said in a rush: "The guy who's been playing Lysander officially has a cold, which means your dad takes center stage tonight!"

"That's great!" Holly said as she passed the florist's shop. The blooms in the window were impossibly colorful. "I mean, for you. Not for the other Lysander."

"Sylvia is coming to the show tonight, so I need to be great. I'm a little nervous. But I think it'll be good. I *hope* it'll be good."

"Hope is a brave thing," said Holly. She felt very wise. Then she added, "I have some news, too." Maybe it was the warmth of the sun, or the sweet, maple-scented air, but telling her dad about the Midsummer festival—*and* all the work she was putting into it—suddenly felt right. "I've actually been planning—"

She paused when she saw a bicyclist coming toward her with a fat stack of newspapers between the handlebars. He whistled as he dropped a few papers in a wire basket by the door of Annie's Market.

"Holly?" her dad said. "What've you been planning?"

"Hold on." Holly grabbed the top paper from the basket. She was eager to see what the *Gazette* had to say about the festival. They'd already mentioned it online, but surely it was front-page-headline material—especially if Beatrice had anything to say about it.

Instead, she found this:

Newcomers Instigating Trouble,
Charles Madison Warns

"Hey, Dad? I have to go."

"But you were saying—"

"Sorry. Talk later."

She hung up. Then, with a sinking feeling, she read on.

Last week's town hall meeting ended with a surprise announcement: the return of the Arden Midsummer festival, last held in 1958 according to Gazette *records. The festival—which will take place in the grove this Saturday afternoon—was announced by twelve-year-old Holly Foster, visiting niece of Vincent Foster, owner of the Arden Antiquarian Shop and a member of the Save the Grove Committee. Given the heavy involvement of the Save the Grove Committee in festival preparations, there's no doubt the event is intended as a protest of sorts against the expansion plans of the Madison Plastics Factory.*

While many locals are excited for the festival, Charles Madison expressed concern in an exclusive interview with the Gazette. *"There's nothing wrong with a festival, especially one that honors Arden's history," Madison says. "But it does give me pause that all this seems to have started with a child interrupting a town hall meeting. A child who doesn't live in Arden, for that matter, and who can't understand its past, present, or future. Come to think of it, most of the Save the Grove Committee members are transplants, including Vincent Foster, Beatrice Quill, and Reggie Summers.*

"While I will always be the first to say that all are welcome in our town, perhaps it would be wise to leave decisions concerning the future of Arden—or the memorialization of its past—in the hands of families who have been here for generations. As a Madison, I'm proud to consider myself a steward of Arden, with the town's best interests always in my heart. . . ."

Holly's blood boiled. She balled up the paper, but the words lingered: *A child who doesn't live in Arden, who can't understand its past, present, or future.*

At first, she was too angry to move or even breathe. She stood statue-still on the sidewalk as shoppers and dogwalkers passed her by. Some of them looked at her a little too long. Maybe some of them had already seen the *Gazette.* And all at once the energy in downtown Arden wasn't warm or bright. It was dark and heavy and wrong.

Holly's breath returned in a rush, hot like steam, and she remembered something Beatrice had told her. *It's going to be a fight to save that grove. Are you ready for a fight?* She was. Now more than ever. And she was ready to take the fight straight to the top.

She turned and ran back down Cornelia Street with the *Gazette* clenched in her fist. When she reached the factory, she threw open the wrought-iron gates, marched up the steps, and burst through the visitors' door.

Ms. Dietrich sat at the reception desk. Behind her, plastic bottles and food containers were displayed on shelves behind glass. On either side of the display were photographs of the factory's construction and portraits of past owners. All Madisons, Holly guessed.

"Holly, are you all right?" said Ms. Dietrich. "Your face is bright red and you look awfully. . . sweaty." She looked around to make sure they were alone, then dropped her voice. "Is this about the Christmas lights? Do you need more?"

"Mr. Madison," Holly panted. "I need to see Mr. Madison."

Ms. Dietrich shifted in her chair. Her voice became curt. "Mr. Madison isn't here yet. May I ask what this is concerning?"

Holly stormed out of the factory, ignoring Ms. Dietrich calling her name behind her. For a minute, Holly stood on the sidewalk, breathing steam and wondering what to do next. Her muscles tensed. She felt rigid as an oak.

He spends half his time at the factory and the other half in his mansion on the hill. That's what Annie had said about Mr. Madison at Holly's first Save the Grove meeting. And then Holly knew. It was time to go to the one place in Arden she hadn't been yet—the one place Lionel hadn't included on the Arden Official Tour.

It was a steep walk up a winding road to the Madisons' manor. The sun beat down. Sweat trickled down Holly's cheeks and her sides cramped, but she didn't slow down until she crested the hill, where the road passed under a gated fence and turned into a private driveway. Unlike the factory gate, this one didn't budge when Holly gave it a push.

Outside the gate, she clutched her side and gulped down air. Behind her, she could see almost all of Arden. There was Uncle Vincent's neighborhood. There was the town square and the grove. From the hilltop, it all looked so small and far away.

Meanwhile, the boxy white manor loomed ahead of her, too bland to be frightening. The blandness only made her angrier. She stuffed the *Gazette* in her back pocket, then stepped up onto the gate. If she couldn't open it, she reckoned she'd just have to climb it.

She imagined what Uncle Vincent might say if he could see her. *Holly, hold on. Slow down. Let's talk this through.*

But Holly didn't want to slow down. She fought with her uncle in her head: *Back off. Leave me alone. Let me do this.* She was spared from fighting the gate, though. As she tried to figure out the best way to climb it, it opened on its own.

Holly hopped to the ground and darted through as a truck rolled down the winding driveway from the manor's garage. She planted her feet on the driveway and lifted her chin, preparing to intercept the truck. . . .

But then, suddenly, it wasn't just Uncle Vincent's voice in her head. It was her own.

What was she *doing*?

Trespassing on private property, for one thing.

Standing directly in the path of a vehicle, for another.

And what, exactly, was she planning to say to the Madisons when she confronted them? That the article in the *Gazette* was mean? Unfair? Untrue? Everything she could imagine saying sounded foolish in her head. Foolish and childish. And wasn't that what the Madisons were accusing her of? Being a foolish child?

She froze, caught between anger and fear. The truck was rounding a bend in the driveway. She didn't think the driver had seen her yet, but any moment now . . .

She jumped behind a cluster of trees. Her foot struck something hard—a skateboard lying discarded in the grass. She bit the inside of her cheek so she didn't yelp, then peeked through the trees so she could see the truck's driver and the passenger without revealing herself.

The passenger was Mr. Madison. The driver was a woman wearing sunglasses and a wide-brimmed hat. It was the same woman Lionel had hidden from outside the florist's shop when he first showed Holly around Arden.

The truck disappeared down the hill and the gate closed behind it with a metallic *clang*. Behind the trees, Holly took long, shuddering breaths. She knew she'd decided to do this; it was her own legs that had carried her here. Still, she felt like she'd been dropped into the middle of a nightmare against her will. And now she had to get out. Now she *really* had to climb that gate.

But something more urgent was weighing on her. She thought about the woman driving the truck. She looked down at the skateboard. The world seemed like a terrible puzzle, and she felt like she was on the verge of piecing it together whether she wanted to or not.

Then she was struck by the uncanny feeling that she was being watched.

She looked at the manor. There was a face in one of the upstairs windows. A boy's face. The boy ducked out of sight as soon as Holly locked eyes with him, but it was long enough to recognize him.

Lionel.

TWENTY

Holly banged on the tall double doors of the Madisons' manor. She was ready to unleash a torrent of accusations on Lionel, but it wasn't Lionel who opened the door. It was Ray, Mr. Madison's teenage son. Holly remembered him from her first visit to Annie's Market.

Ray squinted at her. His spiky hair was askew and there were food stains on his shirt. "That was loud," he drawled.

"I need to see Lionel."

Holly wanted Ray to say "Who's Lionel?" Because then maybe Lionel *didn't* live here. Maybe she *hadn't* really seen his face in the upstairs window.

Instead, Ray said, "Weird. Nobody visits Lionel. But sure."

Holly brushed past him.

The inside of the manor was cavernous but drab—stark white walls, beige furniture, and wall art of skylines and flowers. Holly was sure she'd seen the same pictures in hotel rooms and doctors' offices. In the living room, a gigantic TV was turned to a reality show that involved lots of people in a hot tub yelling at each other. Elise, Mr. Madison's daughter, was lying on the couch. She looked up from her phone. "Aren't you the girl we saw in that little grocery store?"

Holly crossed her arms. "Annie's Market."

Elise sat up. "Wait. You're also the girl Lionel has been hanging out with."

"Where is Lionel? I need to talk to him."

Elise looked at Ray with a smirk. "We *should* tell you to leave. Our parents wouldn't want you here. But that just makes this more fun." She pointed at a spiral staircase. "Upstairs. Third door on the left."

The spiral stairs ended in a long hallway. The third door on the left was closed, so Holly banged on it like she'd banged on the front doors, and when Lionel didn't open it, she said, "I know you're in there!" Still no answer.

"His door doesn't lock, you know."

Holly whipped around. Elise was leaning against a wall nearby. Holly was too annoyed at Elise—at *everything*—to thank her for the tip. She just grunted and flung open the door.

Lionel's room was nothing like the rest of the house. It was an explosion of color—superhero posters and drawings taped to the walls and toys strewn all about the floor. Holly spied action figures, plastic swords, a VR headset, and a pogo stick. Then there were the comic books littering the nightstand and desk. If Lionel had told the truth about cleaning his room—which Holly highly doubted now—she couldn't imagine what it had looked like *before* he cleaned it.

Finding Lionel in the mess was like solving a hidden object puzzle, but soon she spotted his mop of hair poking out from behind a hamper.

"Lionel, I *see* you."

Lionel ran to the door and shut it behind Holly so Elise couldn't see them, then smiled. "Hi, Holly! What brings you here?"

She stared at him in fury and bewilderment. Was he really going to pretend like everything was fine? "You're a Madison." She'd meant to ask it as a question but realized that she didn't need to. It all made sense now—why Lionel never invited her over, why the manor on the hill was the one place that he didn't take her on his Arden Official Tour.

Lionel's smile faded. "Sort of."

"Sort of? What's that supposed to mean?"

He slipped his hands in his pockets and looked down at his toes. "I'm a Madison. But I don't really *feel* like one."

"You lied to me, Lionel."

"I didn't lie. I just . . . didn't tell the whole truth."

Questions sprouted in Holly's mind, prickly as thorns. "Do you even *care* about the grove? Or did you just come to the Save the Grove meetings as a spy? Were you passing everything you heard back to your parents?"

"No!" Lionel said, looking up at her. "I didn't tell my parents anything. I *like* the Save the Grove meetings. Everyone is so nice, and—"

"—and you *did* lie. You lied about needing to clean your room. You lied about having a cold."

"I *did* have to clean my room, the first time I said it. It just got messy again really quick. That always happens." He glanced around his room. Holly didn't know what felt worse—Lionel looking at her or Lionel looking away. "I'm sorry, Holly. *Really* sorry. But someone who works at the factory was at the town hall meeting, and he recognized me even though I was wearing my Leaf Man mask, and he told my parents about it, and my mom told me I couldn't hang out with you anymore—"

"You've been hiding from your parents," Holly said to herself. "That's why you've been acting so weird around town. And when you were giving me the tour of Arden, and you pulled me behind those sunflowers . . ."

"If Mom had seen me hanging up those flyers, she would've been upset. Dad owns the factory, but Mom sort of calls the shots. She's the one who's been really annoyed at the Save the Grove Committee."

Holly thrust the *Gazette* she'd crumpled at Lionel. "So who said all this? Your dad or your mom?"

Lionel slumped as he read the article. "I don't know. I think Mom handles some of Dad's interviews. But either way . . . this isn't fair. They shouldn't have said this about you." He lowered the paper. "I didn't want to tell you about my family because I knew you might not trust me. But I'm not like my parents. I'm not like my brother or sister, either. I don't . . . *fit*." He scrunched up his face in thought. "My parents aren't mean to me. But it feels like . . . like they're floating far away from me. Like even when they're here, they aren't really *here*. And most of the time all they talk about is the factory. Or money."

"But your parents knew you were coming to the Save the Grove meetings, didn't they? They knew you were with Reggie, and Annie, and . . . What do they think you've been *doing* for the last few weeks?"

Lionel shrugged. "They don't ask where I go. They buy me lots of stuff"—he gestured at the sea of toys—"but we don't talk much. They only started caring where I was going when they found out I was hanging out with Mr. V, and . . . you."

"Because I'm such a bad influence." Holly didn't try to keep the bite out of her voice. She aimed each word at

Lionel like an arrow. "Because I'm an outsider, here to stir up trouble."

"You're not a bad influence!" said Lionel, stepping closer to Holly. "You're kind of grumpy sometimes, but in a funny way. I like it. And I've been so bored the last few days, not hanging out with you. Not just bored, but . . . *sad.* I tried to keep busy with my pogo stick, but I broke it, and then I tried to build a blanket fort in the living room, but Elise knocked it over, and . . . Holly, I like being friends with you."

Holly's chest grew hot. She knit her hands together over her heart and pressed hard like she was smothering a fire. "We're *not* friends. I don't need friends, especially friends who lie."

Lionel wilted like a parched flower. "I still don't believe you. Everybody needs friends. But . . . I understand if you don't want to be my friend now."

Holly couldn't stand to look at him anymore, so she looked at the wall behind him. His sketch of Leaf Man was pinned to a bulletin board above his desk. Memories churned. She thought back to her first Save the Grove meeting. When Lionel had showed up, Annie and Beatrice had discouraged Uncle Vincent from letting him in. Holly hadn't understood it at the time, but they were probably worried he'd report back to his parents. She thought about the town hall meeting, too, when Lionel had worn his Leaf

Man mask and Uncle Vincent had asked Lionel if he was sure he wanted to go into the arts center.

"Everyone knew," Holly said quietly. "Everyone but me. They've all been keeping it from me. Even Uncle Vincent."

Lionel sniffed. "Mr. V has always been so nice to me. I don't think he was lying to you. I think he just . . ."

Holly threw the *Gazette* down and made for the door. When she tripped over a plastic sword and banged her knee on Lionel's dresser, she winced but swallowed the pain.

Then she froze. There was a calendar on the wall beside Lionel's door. Her eyes traced the countdown he'd made to her arrival in Arden. He'd crossed out each little square until the day of her flight, where he'd written her name in bright green marker. *Holly.*

And now his voice behind her: "Holly?"

Tears stung her eyes. She shook her head and left his room.

Elise was still in the hallway. She was staring at her phone, but Holly suspected she'd been listening through the door. Holly ignored her and marched down the stairs. She ran into Ray in the living room.

"Uh, are you okay?" he asked.

"Great," said Holly as tears streaked down her cheeks. "Never been better."

He nodded and held out a chip bag. "Cheesy puffs?"

"No cheesy puffs," Holly gritted through her teeth. Then she left the manor, making sure to slam the double doors behind her.

She was out of breath again but didn't pause to catch it. She ran the length of the private driveway, nearly tripping over a discarded scooter, then clambered over the gate. Her sleeve caught on an iron post and ripped. Halfway down the other side of the gate, she lost her footing and fell to the road, scraping her hands. Still, she didn't stop. She *couldn't* stop. Muddled thoughts and awful feelings and hot tears—they were all coming too fast, so she had to be faster. She had to outrace them.

She ran downhill along the winding road. She ran the streets of Arden that Lionel had showed her on his tours. She ran past the town square, and Miss Maisie's Wig Emporium, and Annie's Market. She didn't stop running until she burst through the door of her uncle's shop, a fresh cramp in her side and a new accusation on her lips.

Uncle Vincent was on the phone in his office. He waved at Holly, then took a closer look at her. His brow furrowed. "Just a moment," he mouthed.

Holly waited. Her heart pounded. Her breath rattled. Her eyes landed on the desk at the back of her uncle's shop. As usual, it was covered in old *Gazette*s and weathered books. But there was something else, too.

A small, worn piece of paper.

The 1864 census.

She picked it up. She could tell Uncle Vincent had been working on it. The paper was a little less yellowed, the text a little more legible. It was still hard to see the name that might be hers, but by squinting and holding it up to the light, she could make out the middle letters.

Fowler.

Of course. Those were the first words that popped into her head. Of course, because she'd seen a Fowler tombstone in the Arden cemetery. Of course, because she *knew* her uncle had done a lot of genealogy research and never traced any of their ancestors to Arden. Of course, because the hope had been stupid. She didn't belong in Arden any more than she belonged anywhere else. The town might know her name—her name might even be printed in the *Gazette*—but she was still a stranger. A child who didn't live in Arden and couldn't understand its past, present, or future. What the Madisons had said about her was true, she thought. And if she'd just stuck to her original plan for the summer—if she'd kept to herself, and not talked to anyone, and not gotten involved with anything—none of this would be happening.

Uncle Vincent's voice drifted to her: "When did your great-grandfather live in Arden? And he was a composer, you said? I do have some sheet music that was donated to the shop a while back, but I'd have to check . . ."

She stepped outside and called her dad.

"Hey, Dad, listen—"

"Holly! Are you calling to wish me luck? Because I might need it. Lysander has more lines than I thought."

"I want to leave Arden."

"Oh." A pause. "Really? You said there were still things you wanted to do there. And this morning, you sounded . . . I don't know. Sort of happy."

Familiar faces passed Holly on the sidewalk. Some nodded. Some waved. Over in the town square, a dog peed on the fire hydrant. Holly closed her eyes. When she opened them, everything was blurry and quivering, like she was looking at the world from underwater.

"Holly? Are you there?"

"I'm here," she said. But where was here? *Here* was a tiny town full of weird people who kept secrets from her. *Here* was just a pit stop.

"Did something happen with Vinny?" her dad asked.

"No, it's not him. It's everything. It's nothing. I don't care where I go next. I can come to San Francisco, or go to Mom's house, or . . . or . . . Alaska."

"Actually, about Alaska. I was thinking, and, you know, you were probably right. Money *is* a little tight right now. But maybe in the fall! You could take a week off school, and—"

"Forget Alaska," she snapped. "I just want to leave Arden."

She dropped her voice. "*Please*, Dad."

It was quiet on the other end of the line. Eventually her dad said, "Sure, Holly. Of course. Look, I'm in emergency rehearsals all afternoon before I play Lysander, but I'll call your mom, and we'll look into flights. Maybe we can bring you out here tomorrow, or you can go to Virginia to stay with your mom for a bit. One of us will call you later and figure this out. Okay?"

"Okay."

Click.

"Holly?"

She turned. Uncle Vincent was standing in the door of his shop. "Sorry. I was on the phone with a customer. Is everything okay?"

"I'm leaving Arden," she said. "Tomorrow."

"What?" He stepped onto the sidewalk. "Tomorrow? But what about the Midsummer festival?"

"I'm going back to your house to pack."

"Is this something your parents decided? Can we talk about this? Holly, please wait a second—"

But she was already walking away, following a route she knew by heart but promised herself she'd forget.

TWENTY-ONE

Holly packed.

It wasn't hard. She hadn't brought much to Vermont. The only annoyance was that she'd bothered unpacking in the first place. That she'd hung clothes in the wardrobe, lined up her books on the nightstand, and left both tubes of her prescription toothpaste in the downstairs bathroom cabinet.

Now she gathered up the little pieces of her life and stuffed them back where they belonged: her suitcase, with its faulty zippers and torn lining. She would ask her dad for a new suitcase before their next trip, she decided. One that didn't squeak when she rolled it. The squeaking drove her mad.

She focused her attention on packing. She was good at

packing. She knew how to fold clothes to make them as small as possible and how to layer everything to make the most of the space. It was neat and methodical and almost soothing. She didn't stop when she heard someone enter the house. She didn't let the footsteps on the stairs distract her, either. When Uncle Vincent appeared in her doorway, she only glanced at him long enough to see the *Gazette* clutched in his hand and the worry crinkling his face.

"I saw the paper when I was leaving the shop," he said. "The Madisons were wrong to say this, Holly. They don't speak for the town."

Holly shrugged as she matched her socks. "If you say so."

"I honestly can't believe— They had no right— Going after a *child*, for God's sake."

Usually, Uncle Vincent's sentences faded gently, like he'd gotten lost somewhere along the way. Now each sentence hit a hard stop. Holly saw his jaw clench. She saw his fist tighten around the *Gazette*. And it occurred to her that he was mad. Really mad. Not *at* her, but for her, and she didn't know what to do with that.

"It doesn't matter," said Holly. "I'm leaving and I'm not coming back."

Uncle Vincent's voice softened. "Are you sure you want to leave before the festival? Holly, you've put so much work into it."

"The festival was a dumb idea. It's not going to change anything."

She rummaged beneath the bed for a missing sock. When she turned around, she saw tears on her uncle's face. And now *she* was mad. Who was Uncle Vincent to cry about her leaving? He barely knew her. She'd been in Arden for three and a half measly weeks. That wasn't enough time to get to know each other—let alone care about each other. If he *actually* cared about her, he wouldn't have kept secrets from her.

"Why didn't you tell me that Lionel was a Madison?" she blurted.

Uncle Vincent looked down at the *Gazette*. "Lionel doesn't feel at home in his family. He's a good kid, and . . . I think he's been lonely for a while."

"Being lonely isn't a big deal," said Holly. "Why does everyone act like it's a big deal?"

Uncle Vincent looked at her like he didn't believe her any more than Lionel did. "I'm sorry if it felt like I was keeping something from you. I guess I was. It's just . . . I try to let people introduce themselves, so they can be known the way they want to be known."

"Forget it. I don't care." Holly matched the rogue sock with its partner and folded them into a tight ball.

"I'm also sorry if this hasn't been the summer you

wanted. I know you didn't choose to come here, but I've really enjoyed—"

"Why are you here? The shop doesn't close till six."

"I closed it early. I was worried about you. I *am* worried about you."

"Well, I don't need you to be." She pressed the contents of her suitcase down with both palms, squeezing out as much air as she could. "I'm leaving because I want to leave. Because this town is stupid and I don't like the people here and I don't want to *be* here. Okay?"

She'd landed a hit. She could tell by the way Uncle Vincent winced. And she felt bad for hurting him, but a small part of her was relieved to find that she had the power to hurt anyone.

For a minute, Uncle Vincent lingered on the threshold of her room, forming silent words, stepping toward her and then hesitating. It reminded Holly of when he'd picked her up at the bus stop. Like he didn't know what to do with her.

Now he doesn't have to worry about it anymore, she thought. He could go back to his life, and she could go back to hers, and in a year this whole visit would be a fuzzy memory because that's what happened to memories—they got fuzzy and staticky and eventually they disappeared, the way everything disappears if you just give it time, because nothing lasts.

Finally, he went downstairs. And it felt good to be alone. It felt right—the way of the world, as true as the rising and setting of the sun.

It also felt terrible. She nearly yelled after him to come back so he could keep standing there and she could be mad at him for staying instead of being mad at him for leaving. When his voice drifted up to her a minute later, she wondered if he was calling her down, but soon it became clear he was talking to someone else. She moved to her door and listened.

"Did you already book her flight?" A pause. "That's great about the play, but I want to talk about Holly. I think she's been doing well here. I've loved spending time with her. She's made friends and she's been planning an event for the town. . . . Yes, I know you have rehearsal, but this really can't wait. . . . Yes, but Alex . . . God, Alex, will you *please* stop talking for two seconds and *listen* to me? Alex? Hello?"

Uncle Vincent cursed. The house shivered like the curse was running through all its timbers. Then everything was silent.

Holly realized that she was crying. The tears made her angrier and the anger made her cry more. She shut her door—gently, despite everything—and pressed her forehead against the wood until it hurt. She didn't move until her phone buzzed.

There were several alerts waiting for her. An email from Annie:

> Do you think ten pans of lasagna will be enough for the festival? How about twelve, just to be safe? I think I'll do twelve.

A voicemail from Beatrice: "The *Gazette*'s front page is an outrage! I'm about to march down to the office and give those journalist hacks a piece of my mind. And just wait until I see those Madisons."

Finally, a text from Lionel: I know you're mad at me. I'd be mad at me, too. But I have news about the grove. Like . . . BIG news.

She turned her phone off and threw it on top of her suitcase, then inspected the room. There wasn't anything left to pack. Everything looked just the way it had when she'd arrived. Except for the flowers on the desk—a fresh bundle of hyacinths, the third bouquet that her uncle had put in the vase since she'd arrived. And there, next to the vase, was the maple leaf she'd pocketed her first day in Arden. It was brown and dry now. When she picked it up, it crumbled in her palm.

Soon there would be no trace of her left, she thought—no sign she'd ever been there.

TWENTY-TWO

By dinnertime it was settled. Holly's dad was still busy with his show, but her mom booked her a next-day flight to Virginia. Holly would stay with her stepfamily for a few days, then fly to Florida once her dad was back from San Francisco. "Don't forget your toothpaste!" her mom said.

Holly ate dinner alone in her room that night. It was the same frozen dinner she'd had on her first night at Uncle Vincent's: enchiladas. Since then, her uncle had stocked the freezer with enchiladas. She wondered if he liked them, too. She wondered if he'd eat them when she was gone, or if they would sit there forever, waiting for someone who wasn't coming back. Then she told herself to stop wondering so much. Wondering hurt.

As she carried her empty plate downstairs, she tried to

see the house through a stranger's eyes. But she couldn't. Now she knew which stairs were creaky and the pitch of each creak. She knew the tilt of the wood floor as it sloped from the living room into the kitchen, its color sanded away by generations of footsteps that predated Uncle Vincent. She knew the kitchen sink, too—how the nozzle was mischievous and would shoot water at her face if she wasn't mindful.

She washed her plate, letting the hot water run over her cold hands. The nozzle only attacked her a little bit. She dried the plate with a dishrag and set it in a crowded cabinet.

She still didn't know why Uncle Vincent's kitchen was full of cookware. He hardly ever cooked. There were so many things she hadn't asked him yet. There were so many things she might never ask him now.

On her way back to the stairs, she paused in the living room. Uncle Vincent was watching a painting tutorial, but he wasn't painting. Everything was set up on his tray table—the watercolors, the paper, a mug of water and brushes—but he only stared at the TV as the man with the poofy hair painted clouds over a beach scene.

"My flight is at twelve thirty tomorrow," said Holly. "So I should be at the airport by ten thirty, and if the bus takes almost an hour, I should be at the bus stop by—"

"Nine thirty," said Uncle Vincent.

Holly nodded. She crossed the room and made for the stairs, hurrying past the TV so she didn't block it for long.

"It looks like South Carolina," said Uncle Vincent.

Holly froze on the first step. "That guy's painting?"

"The beaches north of Charleston. That's where I grew up. For a few years, at least."

This rang a faint bell for Holly. She remembered her dad mentioning South Carolina. He'd said it was the most boring place he'd ever lived, a tiny coastal town with nothing to do and nobody to see.

"I liked it there," her uncle said. "I could hear the ocean from our bedroom window." He moved the tray table and stood, then walked to the fireplace and picked up a framed photograph from the mantel. "This was taken at our church in South Carolina. Mom, Dad, Alex, and me."

He handed Holly the picture. She'd glanced at it in passing before. Now she looked closer. Her grandparents stood tall with tight smiles behind the two boys. Her dad was distracted. He was looking off to the side at something Holly couldn't see. A girl, she guessed. He looked like he was about to dart off, but his parents' hands were on his shoulders, holding him in place. Uncle Vincent, meanwhile, looked more serious in his Sunday suit. He was standing to the side, gazing timidly into the camera.

"Sometimes, when I look at these pictures," he said, picking up another off the mantel, "I wonder how young I was when I started feeling alone."

Holly thought she was too mad and sad and tired to feel curious about anything now, but there it was again—curiosity, sprouting up like an unruly weed. "Is that why you left the family?"

"Is that what your dad told you? That I left?" Her uncle squinted at the picture in his hands. "I suppose I did for a while, though I never really planned it that way. I always felt like the odd one out, and when I was old enough to get some space . . . Well, I got some space."

"But why'd you feel like the odd one out? Was it because—" Holly stopped herself.

"Because I'm gay?"

Holly nodded sheepishly.

Uncle Vincent was quiet. Memories seemed to pass over his face. Holly felt like she was watching him age in fast-forward, turning from the boy in the photographs to the man with the salt-and-pepper beard beside her. "Yes, that was part of it," he said slowly. "Not all of it, but part of it. I don't think my parents took it well. We didn't fight about it or anything. They just didn't say much. It was a silence. And the silence . . . got stuck."

"What about my dad?" Holly pressed. "What did he say?"

She was afraid of the answer—afraid of a new reason to be angry with her dad—but her uncle just chuckled. "He was fine. Great, actually. He said he didn't care, told me to live my life. Even tried to set me up with one of his friends." He looked at Holly. "Your dad and I have never been as close as I wish we could be. But I know he cares, in his own way. And I know he loves you more than he's ever loved anyone."

Holly figured her uncle's words should make her feel warm and special, but she just felt confused. She loved her dad. She was *exhausted* by her dad. These truths chased each other around her head in a never-ending game of tag.

"Anyway," said Uncle Vincent, "I didn't visit home for a while after college. I moved around a lot, and . . . I guess a while turned into a longer while."

"How long is a longer while?"

Uncle Vincent scratched his head. "Years, honestly. At some point, I started visiting everyone for holidays again. But it never quite felt natural." He set the picture he was holding back on the mantel. "That's why I feel for Lionel. I know what it's like when home doesn't really feel like home. Or when you feel alone, even when you're with the people you're supposed to be closest to. My family wasn't *bad*, and as much as the Madisons frustrate us, I know they aren't all bad, either. But I don't think your family has to be bad for you to feel . . . a little out of place. A little hurt." He paused, then added, "Maybe more than a little hurt, sometimes."

Holly thought back to something Lionel had told her

when she'd confronted him. *My parents aren't mean to me. But it feels like they're floating far away from me. Like even when they're here, they aren't really* here.

"It's especially hard when you're a kid," her uncle went on, "because you don't get to decide where home is. You're just along for the ride."

Holly's eyes burned. She looked down at the picture in her hands again so Uncle Vincent couldn't see her face. "So why do you have all these pictures?"

"When my parents passed away, I ended up with a lot of their things. Your dad didn't want to take much, and it didn't feel right to throw everything out. For a while these pictures were in a box. I thought I'd leave them there, but one day I took them out and framed a few. My parents and I, we probably weren't the right fit. But I still love them. And I don't want to forget where I come from. It's part of my story."

"Is that where all the stuff in your kitchen came from? Grandma and Grandpa?"

Uncle Vincent laughed. "Yes. I had this idea I'd start cooking. That didn't quite work out."

"The pasta salad was good," said Holly quietly.

She looked at the other photographs on the mantel—different years, different settings, but all similar in certain ways. Her dad always looked like he was about to leap out of the picture and her uncle was always floating to the side, staring into the camera like all the answers might be on the other side of the lens.

"Dad told me you sent him some genealogy stuff," she said.

"It was my hobby for a while. I think I wanted to find some part of the family that I could connect with, even if it was an ancestor."

"Did you?"

"I found records of a great-great-uncle who patented a tea-steeping system. I like to think he and I would have gotten along." Uncle Vincent's eyes twinkled. "I'm glad I got into genealogy, because that's what got me into antiquarianism. I found that I loved discovering old documents and finding stories in them. Then a funny thing happened. I heard an antiquarian in a little town in Vermont was looking for an assistant. Jobs in this line of work don't come up every day, so I packed up everything I had and moved here. To Arden."

He handed Holly another photograph. He was an adult in this one, with a dark, salt-free beard. He was sitting behind the desk at the antiquarian shop next to an old man with wispy hair. "I studied under the shop owner for years until he retired and left the business to me. He passed away last year."

"So that's why you've stayed in Arden all this time? For work?"

"Partly. But also . . . I built a life here. There have never been many dating opportunities"—he blushed—"but I found people I enjoy spending time with. Somewhere along the way it started to feel like home, and those people—Annie, and Beatrice, and others—they started to feel like . . ."

"Family," said Holly.

He seemed to deliberate before speaking again. "I was able to restore that census record—"

"I know. I saw it on your desk today."

He frowned. "I was hoping to talk to you about it. I wanted to say . . . It would've been fun to find a family connection here. I got the sense that you were excited about it. I was a little excited, too, even though I knew it was unlikely. But our family doesn't have to come from Arden in order for us to belong in Arden."

"But you heard everyone at the town hall meeting," said Holly. "They were arguing about whose family had lived in Arden the longest. That's why the Madisons have their name on everything. Because they've been here so long."

Uncle Vincent raised an eyebrow. "The Madisons put their name on everything because they have money. And everyone who was arguing at the town hall meeting . . . If you go far enough back, all their families are from somewhere else. Arden was only established in the 1700s. In the grand scheme of history, that's not so long ago. Indigenous people have been on this continent for tens of thousands of years."

Holly nodded and hugged her arms to her chest. "I guess I just felt like if we were from here, somehow, then . . . then maybe I would've had a reason to bring back the festival and save the grove. Maybe I wouldn't have been an outsider."

Uncle Vincent looked at her for a long time. She wondered what he saw. "I think that, for me, belonging means sharing what you have to offer," he said. "And accepting what others offer, too. Sometimes that second part is the trickiest. So . . . in my book, you belong here as much as any of us." He paused, then added quickly, "I'm not saying you have to feel like you belong here. But if that *is* how you feel, or if that's how you feel about some other place you find someday . . . I just want you to know that I think you get to decide where you belong."

Holly's chest tightened. She set the picture in her hands back on the mantel. "I know what you're trying to do. But you don't know how I feel. You don't know *me*."

Uncle Vincent looked at her the same way he looked out of the photographs on the mantel—like he was looking for something just out of sight, or reaching for something just out of reach. "You're right. There's a lot I don't know about you. But I do know some things. I think I understand some of them, too. Maybe not completely. But a little bit, at least.

And I'd be glad to know you better, if you'd help me try."

Holly's heart felt like a tangled knot. She wanted to scream at Uncle Vincent. She wanted him to pull her into a hug, too—the hug he hadn't given her when he picked her up from the bus stop three and a half weeks ago. Where had that hug gone?

There was a knock on the front door. Holly was grateful for the interruption. She ran halfway up the stairs, then watched from the shadows of the stairwell as Uncle Vincent opened the door. She heard the knocker's voice before she saw him.

"Hi, Mr. V! Is Holly home?"

Uncle Vincent glanced over his shoulder. His eyes caught Holly's. She shook her head and shrank deeper into the shadows.

"Holly isn't up to visitors right now, I'm afraid," Uncle Vincent told Lionel.

Holly crept up the rest of the stairs and slipped into her room. She closed her door behind her, shutting out their voices. Shutting out everything.

She looked at the clock on the nightstand. It was just past nine o'clock. Too early for bed, and she hadn't brushed her teeth yet, but she couldn't stand the thought of leaving her room again. So she changed into her pajamas—she'd left them at the top of her suitcase for easy access—and slipped under the covers. She thought about reading, but all her books were packed, and anyway, she didn't want to read. She didn't want to think. She just wanted to sleep. She turned off the lamp and burrowed into the dark.

Except it wasn't totally dark. She saw pinpricks of starlight through the windows. And she'd muffled her uncle and Lionel, but it wasn't silent. She heard crickets and frogs and the hoot of an owl somewhere in the night.

Then there was her heart. She heard it beating. Her whole body shook with it. She lay as still as she could, but she had the breathless feeling that she was running. She didn't know what she was running toward or running from, only that it was urgent. Far too urgent for rest.

For hours she tossed and turned, images of silvery trees and branching roots and white, lacy fungi flickering behind her eyelids. The longer she was awake, the more she strained after sleep, but sleep never came. All the while, the birches outside rustled in the wind, their voices hushed but insistent.

At last, she threw off her sheets. "Ugh," she said. "Fine."

With the feeling that she was moving through a dream, she tugged on her shoes and padded down the stairs, avoiding the creaky spots. She didn't know where she was going, or why; she supposed she was caught in some kind of sleep-deprived delirium, but her feet seemed to know the way.

The door to Uncle Vincent's bedroom was cracked. She

paused to make sure he was snoring, then tiptoed past his room on her way out of the house. Sometimes the front door groaned when it opened, but it was silent now. Holly whispered a thank-you to the house and slipped outside.

The first light of dawn was painting the town purply-orange. Holly rubbed her arms—it was colder than she'd expected—then took a long, slow breath of the new day and began the walk toward the grove.

TWENTY-THREE

The streets were quiet and the houses were dark. Arden was still sleeping. In dawn's half-light, the town felt both familiar and strange. Holly looked at the homes and storefronts and wondered: Was Arden the town of Mr. and Ms. Madison, where newcomers were expected to keep their mouths shut? Or was it the town of Uncle Vincent and Reggie and Beatrice and Annie, where a girl just visiting for the summer could try to save a grove of trees? She wasn't sure.

She was relieved when she reached the grove. Whatever the town might think of her, she felt at ease as soon as she was surrounded by the trees. They loomed around her and towered over her, but they didn't frighten her, and anyway, she knew her way around the grove now. She was glad to see it one more time before she left.

When she found the tree with the crescent moon roots, she curled up in a bed of leaves by its base, letting the roots encircle her. It felt more comfortable than her bed, somehow, and for the first time all night, a stillness came over her. Her heart still raced, but the burden of it felt lighter, like maybe the roots that were bearing the tree were bearing her, too.

With her head nestled in the crook of her elbow, she watched dawn slowly illuminate the grove. Sunlight spread over the ground like soft fire and lit up the roots of the arden trees one by one. Soon the entire root network lay shimmering around Holly in the morning light, dotted with dew-speckled mushrooms that hinted at the fungal network woven tightly through every fiber of the soil. The lights that she and Uncle Vincent had strung between the branches became visible, too, along with the piles of folding tables and chairs that still had to be set up for the festival. When the sun touched her skin, it kindled a warmth in her chest that spread through her and invited her to sink deeper into the leaves.

She wondered what would happen to the grove after she left. Would it be cut down by summer's end? And even if not, would it survive much longer?

She thought about what Logan had said. Trees were sensitive but resilient, too. She'd come to the same conclusion in her sixth-grade science report. Trees could adapt. They could persevere. Especially when they weren't alone. When they were plugged into the root and fungal network, they relied on each other for support. And the arden trees had more than each other now. They had the Save the Grove Committee, plus Susan, Pritha, and Logan, all trying to figure out how to save them. Maybe it wasn't too late.

Not that it matters. I'll be gone. I don't have to care anymore. I never should've cared in the first place.

But the voice in her head was a whisper, already fading. Maybe it was the sleepless night, or maybe it was the strangeness of lying in the grove in her pajamas, but it was suddenly easy for Holly to admit it to herself: she cared about the grove, and she would keep caring about the grove after she was gone. The trees' survival mattered whether she was in Arden or not. It mattered to her uncle, and the committee, and the town, and the foresters, and the earth. It mattered to her.

Her heart ached, but here, curled up among the roots, seemed like a safe place to ache. And was aching such a bad thing, anyway?

She closed her eyes. Her mind wandered. She remembered learning in Ms. Wilkins's science class about how leaves opened their special pores, called stomata, to let in carbon dioxide so they could photosynthesize. She felt a bit like a photosynthesizing leaf now. She imagined her skin was porous, every cell breathing in the oxygen that the trees produced as her lungs exhaled the carbon dioxide that the trees needed. How did it all work so beautifully?

One image morphed into the next. She pictured her fingers and toes and every strand of her hair tying into the root system of the arden trees. Then she pictured the root system extending beyond the grove, running beneath every part of the town, connecting Uncle Vincent and Beatrice and Annie and Reggie and Lionel and *everyone*, even Mr. and Ms. Madison and Ray and Elise. And farther still, to the Vermont Technical Institute, where arden trees were being studied in labs and grown in a greenhouse. Maybe all the way to Virginia, or Florida, or San Francisco. And all of it starting here, in the grove, right where Holly lay.

Impossible, she thought. *Foolish. DEFINITELY unscientific.* But that voice was a fading whisper, too. In its place came Uncle Vincent's voice, quiet but strong: *I think you get to decide where you belong.*

Holly checked her phone for the time. Uncle Vincent would be waking up soon. She needed to go back and get ready for the day ahead—the car ride to the bus stop, the bus to the airport, and the two flights that would carry her to Virginia.

She stood and brushed leaves and dirt off her pajamas. Then she stretched, lifting her arms over her head and standing as tall as she could. Not nearly as tall as the old arden trees, but still, tall. Taller than a sapling. Taller than she'd ever been before. She supposed that was how growing worked. Still, it felt a bit wondrous.

She waited for her feet to start moving.

Instead, they dug down into the soil.

Go, Holly told herself.

But she stayed.

She wasn't sure what she was doing. All she knew was that she had to call her dad. She didn't know what she was going to say until he picked up, his voice bleary with sleep. "Holly? It's super early on the West Coast."

"I'm not flying back today," she said. "I'm staying in Arden, at least for today and tomorrow. There's an event I've been planning, and I need to be here for it."

"But your mom already booked your flight!" Her dad sounded alert now. She pictured him sitting up in bed and rubbing sleep out of his eyes. "And yesterday you seemed so ready to leave."

"I'm not flying back today," she repeated, for her dad and for herself.

"Well, if you're sure. . . . Is everything okay with Vinny? He called yesterday and he seemed kind of weird. Weird and grumpy."

Holly smiled to herself. "He's good. It's all good."

"You're going to have to call your mom. She has all your flight information."

"Okay, I'll call her," said Holly. And she did. Her mom didn't pick up, but Holly left a message, apologizing for changing her mind but insisting that she absolutely, one hundred percent had to stay in Arden a little longer.

Then she dialed another number, one she'd already memorized without meaning to.

"Holly?"

"Hi, Lionel."

"Are you really calling me or am I dreaming? Because I had a dream you called me, but then I woke up, and you hadn't called. But now you're really calling me, except I don't know if you're really calling me, because what if I'm—"

"I'm really calling you. Can you meet me at Uncle Vincent's?"

"When?"

"Now. And Lionel?"

"Yeah, boss?"

"Bring your big news."

TWENTY-FOUR

Holly blazed through town in her pajamas. By the time she reached her uncle's street, the sun had cleared the horizon and Arden was stirring to life. Neighbors watered rosebushes and walked tongue-lolling dogs. Joggers passed Holly on morning runs while cars rumbled downhill toward the factory. Holly waved to everyone who waved at her but kept moving, climbing the stairs that led up the sloping yard of the blue house on the hill. Just as she reached the landing, Uncle Vincent flung open the door. Relief washed over his face.

"I was just calling your dad. I went to wake you, but you weren't— I thought maybe— But your suitcase—"

"I'm not going home," she announced. "Not today, at

least. I'm staying for the festival."

Uncle Vincent broke into a smile. It occurred to Holly that there was always an element of surprise to her uncle's smile, like the cosmos had just handed him an unexpected gift. "That's wonderful," he said. "I mean, if that's what you want."

"It is," said Holly.

"Did you talk to your—"

"I just talked to Dad and left a message for Mom."

Uncle Vincent looked at his phone. "Ah, your dad is calling me back now. And . . ." He looked past Holly. "I believe you have a visitor."

Holly turned to find Lionel coming up the steps behind her. He paused to sniff the blossoms in one of her uncle's flowerbeds, then scurried up the rest of the way.

While her uncle stepped back into the house with his phone—"Everything's fine. . . . Yes, I just talked to her. . . ."—Holly stared at Lionel. He stood in front of her, shifting his weight from foot to foot like he was doing a little dance.

"Hi," he said.

"Hi," she said. There was a little bite to the word. She was still mad at Lionel. But she was happy to see him, too. This felt paradoxical to Holly. Paradoxes were confusing. In her confusion, she didn't know what to say.

Luckily, Lionel always had something to say. "So I've been thinking, and I want to help with the festival, and I want to *go* to the festival, even if my parents don't like it. Because it's worth it. It's the most worth-it thing ever.

"And I shouldn't have lied to you about having a cold, even though I *did* have the sniffles. I shouldn't have lied to you about needing to clean my room, either, even though it was true the first time I said it. I should've just told you the whole truth, even if it would've made you hate me and never speak to me again."

"I wouldn't have stopped speaking to you," Holly said. The words wobbled. "Well . . . okay. Maybe I would've. I'm still mad at you for lying to me. Even if I sort of understand why you did." Paradox after paradox. Holly's brain hurt.

"Sooo . . . We can be friends again?"

Friends. The word poked at Holly. Saying *friends* was planting a flag in the ground. It was a declaration. A commitment. A binding.

But even as she stood on the landing of Uncle Vincent's house, part of her was still in the grove, lying on a bed of leaves, imagining her roots growing deep into the earth and tying her to every tree, every person, every piece of Arden. So even though it scared her, and even though part of her was still mad at Lionel, she said, "We can be friends. Again."

The sudden delight on Lionel's face was hard to bear, like a too-hot sun. Holly hurried on. "You said you have big news about the grove."

Lionel nodded. "BIG news," he said. "I tried to come and tell you last night, even though I knew you were super mad at me. But Mr. V said you weren't feeling so great. Then I thought about telling *him* the news, but I really wanted you to hear it first, so—"

"Well?" Holly said. "What is it?"

Lionel looked up and down the street, then peeked around the corner of Uncle Vincent's house. Satisfied, he dropped his voice to a whisper. "I went down to the kitchen yesterday morning to get gummy worms from the pantry because I like gummy worms and peanut butter for breakfast, and my dad's laptop was on the kitchen island, but my dad was in the bathroom, and I know I *shouldn't* have looked at his screen, but it was right there, so I took a peek, and . . ."

"And?" said Holly.

Lionel leaned in closer. Holly could smell his peanut-butter-and-gummy-worms breath. "Dad was writing an email. It must've been to someone at the factory. It was confusing at first, but I scrolled through the email chain and figured out what was going on. The factory has been dumping some kind of chemical waste in the grove. For years. In the email, Dad wrote that the grove has to be cut down ASAP. That means *as soon as—*"

"I know what ASAP means," said Holly.

"Me too! So, he said the grove has to be cut down ASAP, before the foresters from that school find out what's going on."

At first Holly only felt anger, the kind that starts as a fire in your chest and spreads to every finger and toe until your whole body burns like a star going supernova. She didn't know much about chemical waste disposal, but she knew it wasn't okay to dump anything toxic in nature. Who would do such a thing? And *why*? Didn't they care about the environment at all? What was *wrong* with people?

Then her anger made a little room for inquisitiveness—the part of her mind that solved puzzles. And Lionel's news was the missing puzzle piece.

"*That's* why the grove is dying," she said, pacing the landing. "I thought it might've been air pollution—you know, all that junk coming out of the factory smokestacks. But that didn't make sense, because that smoke goes *everywhere.* If that was the cause, it would hurt all the trees around town, not just the grove. But these chemicals they're dumping, they probably seep into the soil and the creek."

Another piece snapped into place. "Wait. *That's* why the factory wants to build the visitors' center and museum there! It didn't really make sense to me before. They could build it anywhere, so why there? But if they tear down the grove, it's like . . . destroying the evidence. They're trying to hide what they've done." She stopped pacing. "Lionel, this changes everything. But are you sure? I mean, that's definitely what you saw in those emails?"

"Cross my heart and hope to die!" said Lionel. "Except, I really don't want to die." He pulled out his phone. "I took pictures of my dad's computer screen. See?"

Holly flicked through the images, squinting to read the email text.

"And actually, on my way here—" Lionel began, but Holly wasn't listening.

"We have to tell Uncle Vincent about this," she said. "Now."

"Okay, but I should tell you—"

"Come on!"

They hurried inside. Uncle Vincent was in his room talking to Holly's dad on the phone. Holly waited anxiously for him to finish. She could only hear snippets of the conversation—something about the grove, and the festival, and her name over and over again: *Holly.*

Holly's heart tremored. People talking about her always unsettled her. She thought about the note that her sixth-grade guidance counselor had written to her dad: *Holly shows a strong aptitude for science, but she's struggling to find her social footing.* She thought about the interview with Mr. Madison in the *Gazette*: *But it does give me pause that all this seems to have started with a child interrupting a town hall meeting. A child who doesn't live in Arden, for that matter. . . .*

Then she remembered her uncle's anger at the Madisons after he'd read the article. She remembered the way his face had lit up just now when she told him she wasn't leaving today. And she decided that she trusted her name with him—trusted that, whatever he was saying about her, he was in her corner.

When Uncle Vincent hung up, he joined Holly and Lionel in the living room.

"Is everything okay?" Holly asked. "What did he say?"

"Oh, this and that," said Uncle Vincent airily. "It seems he's taken a starring role in *A Midsummer Night's Dream* for a few nights."

"Oh, that's right!" Holly made a mental note to ask her dad how his Lysander performance was going, but right now there were more urgent things on her mind. With a little help from Lionel, she explained to her uncle how the factory was polluting the grove.

For several minutes, Uncle Vincent examined the pictures Lionel had taken of his dad's emails. Holly grew impatient waiting for him to say something. "This is big, right?" she said when she couldn't wait any longer. "If we took this to the town council, it could change things, couldn't it?"

"Maybe," said Uncle Vincent. "But . . . we can't do that."

"What? Why not?"

Uncle Vincent exhaled slowly. "These are private emails. There would be questions about how we found them. We could try to keep our source anonymous, but there's a chance this could implicate Lionel. And we're not going to risk that."

But we have to do SOMETHING with this! Holly nearly screamed. *This is HUGE!* It took every ounce of self-restraint she could muster to keep quiet. And in the quiet, she decided glumly that Uncle Vincent was right. Lionel had taken a big risk in sharing this news with her. He'd be taking a much bigger risk if they brought this to the council. As much as she hated to admit it to herself, they couldn't ask Lionel to do that.

"Actually . . ." said Lionel.

Holly and Uncle Vincent stared at him. Somehow, he managed to look both sheepish and devious at the same time.

"Actually . . . ?" Holly pressed.

"That's what I was trying to tell you just now, Holly," said Lionel. "I printed the pictures, and on my way here, I dropped them in an envelope outside Beatrice's door."

"Beatrice?" said Holly and Uncle Vincent at the same time.

Lionel nodded. "I thought she'd know what to do with them. But don't worry! I didn't put my name on the envelope or anything, and I didn't let her see me. I was very stealthy. Like a superspy."

Uncle Vincent jumped into action, dialing a number and setting his phone on the coffee table. A few moments later, Beatrice's voice crackled through the speaker for all to hear. "Vincent! I was going to call *you*, as a matter of fact. You'll never guess what I discovered this morning. You'll read all about it in the *Gazette* soon, but I'll tell you now that—"

"You already took the photos to the *Gazette*?"

"How do *you* know about the photos? But yes, I'm leaving the *Gazette*'s office now. And I already sent a copy to the council, too!"

Uncle Vincent rubbed his forehead. "Oh no. Oh, dear."

"*Oh dear* is right," said Beatrice. "That's exactly what the Madisons will be saying soon!"

With a promise to talk more later, Uncle Vincent quickly hung up. "Lionel," he said, "that was *incredibly* reckless." Then, more quietly: "And brave."

Lionel looked down at his hands. Slowly, he traced the lines of his palm with a finger. "I love my parents. But . . . I don't like what they're doing at the factory. It just isn't right. I think the town should know about this."

"If your parents find out you took those pictures, will you be okay?" Holly asked. Suddenly—and surprisingly—Lionel being okay felt like the most important thing in the world to her. More important than the town finding out about the pollution. More important than the Midsummer festival. More important than anything.

"They might ground me for ever and ever. But they never really yell at me or anything. They hardly talk to me at all."

"If you ever *aren't* okay, you know you can talk to me," said Uncle Vincent. "You know you can come here."

Lionel smiled. "I know, Mr. V."

Holly nodded. "So . . . if the news is out—or about to be out—what do we do now?"

"I'm going to have a word with the *Gazette* and make sure they don't print anything that implicates Lionel," said Uncle Vincent. "I don't want those pictures included in any articles. But . . . I suppose you can let Dr. Morales know about this. If she's studying samples from the grove, she might be finding her own evidence of the pollution."

Holly dialed Susan at once. In her head, she started planning her voicemail message. She figured Susan was too busy being a brilliant scientist to answer her phone, so Holly was surprised when she heard Susan's clipped voice. "Yes?"

"Hi, Dr. Morales. This is—"

"Holly. I was going to call you today."

"You were?"

"Interesting results from the tests we ran on the samples from your grove." Holly put Dr. Morales on speakerphone. "There are alarming levels of several industrial chemicals in the soil and the water. Benzene, xylene, and toluene, to name a few. Looks like the chemicals have entered the arden trees through the roots. Those trees aren't dying of anything natural. They're—"

"Being poisoned," said Holly. "I know. Dr. Morales, we have proof that the plastics factory has been dumping chemical waste in the grove for a long time."

"What kind of proof are we talking about?"

"Emails between people at the factory," said Lionel. "Also, hi. This is Lionel."

"Dr. Morales, this is Vincent, Holly's uncle. Can you share those lab results with us? Given what we've learned, I think we should take up the case with the town council again, and I'd rather use your results than these emails."

"You bet," said Susan. "I was already planning on having another word with your councilmembers myself."

"So you think there's still a chance to save the grove?" Holly said.

"This isn't my first rodeo when it comes to conservation. I've seen it go both ways. Prepare for the worst but fight for the best." Dr. Morales groaned. "My daughter is drawing on the wall again. Vincent, I'll call you later and we'll make a plan for approaching the council together. And Pritha, Logan, and I will see you all tomorrow at that festival you're planning. Rosalie, put down that marker RIGHT NOW!"

Click.

Holly looked from Uncle Vincent to Lionel, her body humming. She was surprised how awake she felt after a sleepless night. "What now?"

"I have a few calls to make," said Uncle Vincent, "and I'm late opening the shop. As for the two of you . . . Well, there's still a festival to plan!"

"Oh," said Holly. "Right." Nerves wriggled through her like peanut-butter-covered gummy worms. "There's still so much to do."

Lionel grinned and saluted her. "At your service, boss."

TWENTY-FIVE

Holly changed out of her pajamas, brewed three mugs of Irish Breakfast tea—one for her, one for Lionel, and one for her uncle—then called her mom. Her flight was refundable for credit, as it turned out, and her mom was appeased by Holly's promise to visit Virginia later in the summer. With that settled, and at least a bit of caffeine coursing through her veins, Holly walked downtown with Lionel on her heels.

"Aren't you worried about your parents seeing you with me?" Holly said as they passed the florist's shop.

"They're both at the factory this morning," said Lionel. "I'm free as a bird!" Still, Holly noticed Lionel looking around furtively at every street corner and tucking himself behind streetlamps and garbage cans as he followed her.

Either he *was* worried about running into his parents or he was practicing his superspy skills. He seemed to be enjoying himself, at least.

They found Annie in the kitchen at the back of her market, baking up a storm. Sweat glistened on her forehead and matted her hair to her rosy cheeks. "Where did all the time go?" she cried as she checked the temperature of a loaf of banana bread in the oven. "I still have seven loaves to bake for the festival, and we need more lasagnas, and I have to interview someone in . . ." She brushed flour off her wristwatch. "Thirteen minutes!"

Holly pressed her back to the wall as Annie whirled through the kitchen like a tornado. "I'm thinking we should have Save the Grove swag bags to hand out at the festival," Annie went on. "I ordered more supplies. They're sitting by the register, but I don't know when I'm going to find time—" The bell over the market door pealed. Annie poked her head outside the kitchen and groaned. "The guy I'm interviewing is"—she checked her watch again—"twelve minutes early!"

Holly wiped a smudge of butter off Annie's arm, then shepherded her out of the kitchen. "You handle the interview. Lionel and I will watch the register and make swag bags."

"And be taste testers," Lionel said, dipping his fingers in a bowl of banana bread batter.

So while Annie interviewed a sharply dressed man at a

sidewalk table outside the market, Holly and Lionel took care of customers who came in for pastries and fresh-brewed coffee. When they weren't busy ringing people up, they had a swag bag race rematch. Lionel beat Holly by two swag bags, but Holly insisted Lionel had only won because she'd taken a break to refill the coffeepot. Holly helped herself to the coffee, too. She expected the first sip to be sweet relief after weeks of tea but actually found herself missing the taste of ginger and turmeric.

When Annie brought the interviewee inside the market and showed him around, Holly eavesdropped. The man explained to Annie that he'd only recently arrived in Arden. His partner had taken a job at the factory. Now he was looking for work of his own—and a way to use his culinary school degree.

"You should come to the festival tomorrow," said Holly, handing him one of the flyers that Uncle Vincent had made. "It'll be a good way to get to know the town."

"Plus, it's probably going to be the greatest thing ever," said Lionel.

"This looks fun," the man said. Then, to Annie: "Uh, do those kids work here?"

"No, no," said Annie with a laugh. "Well . . . sometimes."

As payment for their half hour of work, Annie gave Holly and Lionel a box of maple scones and two iced teas when the man left.

"He seemed nice," said Holly.

"Does he know how to make scones?" Lionel added. "That feels important."

"Oh, I don't know," said Annie, tidying a shelf of canned soups. "He's a possibility."

"A possibility sounds like progress," said Holly.

Annie looked Holly in the eye for the first time that morning. "You're right. It is." She checked her watch once again. "Don't let me keep you two here all day. I'm sure you have lots to do. Tomorrow's the big day!"

So, after splitting the scones—Lionel took the last one as a prize for his swag bag victory—Holly and Lionel grabbed their iced teas and headed for their second stop of the day: Miss Maisie's Wig Emporium.

Today Miss Maisie wore a long teal wig that made Holly think of mermaids. Before talking festival business, Miss Maisie insisted that Holly and Lionel pick out wigs, too. "One doesn't enter a wig emporium and *not* try on wigs," she said. Holly wondered if this was one of Miss Maisie's Fundamental Truths of Life.

Lionel ran through the store, trying on wigs of every style and color before landing on poofy blond waves with a headband. "Do I look like a rock star?" he asked, admiring his reflection in a mirror.

No, Holly thought. "Maybe," she said.

Holly didn't make any moves to pick out a wig, so Miss

Maisie selected one for her—a short black bob—then stood her in front of the mirror next to Lionel. Holly was alarmed and pleased by her reflection. She wondered if this was how her dad felt when he put on a costume for the first time. Like, for a little while at least, he could be anyone.

"Every day is a chance for reinvention," Miss Maisie whispered. Then she snatched the wigs off their heads. "On to the festival!"

She handed Holly a stack of labels with the names of various Arden businesses that would be attending the festival, along with a drawing she'd made on the back of a receipt. "All the businesses want their own table at the festival so they can advertise and sell merchandise. But the tables have to be set up *exactly* this way." She tapped a finger on the receipt drawing, which Holly now saw was a table arrangement.

"Why?" Holly asked.

"I really shouldn't say. But if you absolutely *insist*, I'll tell you. I have to warn you, though, it's all very scandalous." Miss Maisie leaned in conspiratorially. "Remember how Mr. Wilson from the record shop and Mr. Butler from the cat massage parlor split? Well, ever since the breakup, they can't be near each other." She stared at Holly and Lionel expectantly. Holly did her best to look shocked and elbowed Lionel until he did the same.

"I *know*," said Miss Maisie. "And that's not all. Ms.

Derry, who owns the bagel shop, refuses to be next to her twin, Ms. Bolin, the fortune teller. Apparently, Ms. Bolin gave Ms. Derry a *terrible* fortune when they were both seven years old. Haven't said a word to each other since."

"I like Ms. Bolin," said Lionel. "She predicted I'd get roller skates. Then I did."

Holly sighed. "Fine. Lionel and I will set up the tables and label them."

Suddenly, muffled saxophone filled the emporium. Miss Maisie's face soured but Lionel grinned. "Reggie!"

Holly and Lionel said goodbye to Miss Maisie, reassuring her that they had indeed been very shocked by the town gossip, then checked in on Arden's blue jazz sensation. Reggie was working on his setlist for his festival performance, trying out different arrangements of songs. Lionel had advice: "Play the biggest, coolest song last. And maybe get some fireworks that'll launch behind you when you finish. I saw that on TV once."

"No fireworks in the grove," said Holly.

"Oh," said Lionel. "That makes sense."

Holly confirmed details with Reggie—when he would play, and when he should set up in the morning. Then it was time for lunch. Holly and Lionel picked up three sandwiches from Annie's and brought one to Uncle Vincent at his shop.

"Have you talked to Susan again?" Holly asked.

"Not yet," said Uncle Vincent, "but she emailed me the lab results and said she'd call this afternoon."

"Do you think she'll really come to the festival? Logan and Pritha, too?" Holly didn't ask the question that was really nagging at her: Would *anyone* come to the festival? It seemed like all of Arden was excited about the event, but Holly still feared it would be a flop. It felt safer to ask about the foresters than the whole town, though.

"I think so," her uncle said. "Didn't Susan say they would?"

Holly was skeptical. Her dad often *said* he would do things—drive her to school so she didn't have to ride the bus; decorate their latest home; book a trip to Alaska—but he didn't always actually *do* them. Adults were slippery sometimes. "We'll see," she said.

Uncle Vincent studied her. "Holly, are you nervous about the festival?"

"No," said Holly emphatically, but she had the annoying suspicion that both her uncle and Lionel could tell when she was lying. "I mean . . . maybe a little." She spoke quickly then: "What if it rains? What if it's too hot? And I still don't know how I'm going to explain the tree-listening tradition to everyone. We hardly have any information about it!"

"Ah," said Uncle Vincent. "Well, let's see. The trees will offer shelter from rain or heat. As for listening to the trees . . . Whatever we don't know, we can fill in, can't we?

We can make a new tradition together."

"Everyone can pretend to be Leaf Man!" said Lionel. "He can talk to trees, remember?"

Uncle Vincent laughed. "That's one way to do it. Or we can keep it simple. I still think it's a lovely idea—listening to the trees, inviting them to listen to us . . ."

"I think so, too," said Holly. And she liked the idea of making a new tradition together.

After lunch it was time for Holly and Lionel's final task of the day: setting up the fold-out tables and chairs in the grove. In addition to the tables for Arden businesses—which had to be carefully arranged per Miss Maisie's back-of-a-receipt map—they needed tables for food, swag bags, and Reggie's music equipment.

While they worked beneath the trees, the man with the bowler hat snuck past them, startling Holly. He tucked a small slip of paper in the crevice of an arden tree, then whipped around and looked at them accusingly. "Don't watch! You'll spoil the scavenger hunt!" Holly and Lionel failed to stifle their laughter.

It was late afternoon when they finished arranging the tables and chairs. The fatigue of a sleepless night and a busy day hit Holly as they collapsed on a bench in the town square. In a daze, she watched shopkeepers wrapping up for the day. Window signs were flipped from Open to Closed. Keys were turned in locks.

"Won't your parents be leaving the factory soon?" Holly asked.

Lionel swung his legs beneath the bench. "Yeah. I should go home. But . . . a few more minutes."

"Okay. A few more minutes." Holly closed her eyes and rested her head on the back of the bench. She'd always felt like she was bad at doing nothing. Usually, doing nothing was just an invitation for her heart to race. But now a stillness washed over her, and it felt good to do absolutely nothing. Really good.

Until Lionel poked her. "Wanna play catch?"

Holly peeped open an eye. "Well," she said, "okay."

So they stood a few yards apart in the middle of the square and tossed Lionel's bouncy ball back and forth. Each time it arced over their heads, it crossed the sun and glinted in the golden afternoon light. Holly imagined it was a shooting star falling into her hands, and she didn't even feel silly for it.

TWENTY-SIX

The morning of Midsummer's Eve dawned misty and cool. As Holly and Uncle Vincent left the blue house on the hill, the mist glowed in the early light and made Holly shiver—though it might've been nerves, too. Her pulse ran light and quick like a stone skipped over water.

Uncle Vincent stifled a yawn as they descended the steps that led down to the street. "Last night Susan and I drafted a letter to the town council with her lab results."

Holly's pulse skipped faster. "You'll tell me what you hear? Even if I'm gone then?"

Her uncle seemed surprised by the question. "Of course."

They met the rest of the Save the Grove Committee in the grove for final preparations before the festival officially began at noon. Equipment had to be unloaded from

Reggie's van and placed in the clearing where he would perform. The trunk of Annie's car was full of lasagnas and baked goods—these had to be set up buffet-style on the fold-out tables in the grove—plus swag bags. Beatrice, meanwhile, shuffled around with Henry and offered criticisms: the desserts should be placed to the right of the lasagnas, not the left. Reggie's speakers should be angled just so for better sound; didn't he know *anything* about acoustics?

The new members of the committee arrived early, too. While Miss Maisie set up her table—a tribute to her emporium, with a selection of her most daring wigs—the man in the bowler hat did a final review of his scavenger hunt. Even Ms. Dietrich showed up to make sure she'd provided enough string lights for the festival. When the lights were plugged into the generator, they twinkled like fairies between the mist-draped trees.

There was only one committee member missing. Again and again, Holly looked for Lionel. He'd told her he would be at the festival even if his family didn't like it. But what if his parents didn't let him leave the house? Holly imagined Lionel under lockdown—chains across his bedroom door, a chair wedged beneath the knob. Maybe she'd have to stage a rescue. The idea was a little thrilling but mostly concerning. She didn't want to climb that gate again.

Finally, everything was set up for the festival and there

was nothing to do but wait. It was nearly noon. A tense silence fell over the committee. Not even the trees stirred. And now, without tasks to keep her busy and quiet her mind, Holly felt a fresh wave of anxiety.

She looked at each Save the Grove Committee member in turn. They'd all put so much effort into the festival. *She'd* put so much effort into the festival. Fears bubbled: What if the Madisons' article in the *Gazette* had convinced everyone not to come? Or worse, what if nobody cared about the grove enough to show up? Maybe the forest that had once meant so much to Arden had truly been forgotten. Maybe nothing could save it now.

With a pit in her stomach, Holly looked at Uncle Vincent. He smiled and tapped his ear. At first, Holly didn't know why. Then she heard it, too. The crunch of footsteps on fallen leaves. She followed the sound and saw a family making their way through the trees toward the clearing. A young boy tugged on his mom's arm. "Look at the lights," he said. The father patted his belly. "Smell the *food*!"

Behind the family were others: The elderly couple who handed out religious pamphlets in the town square. The woman from the town hall meeting who had complained about the broken air-conditioning at the post office. The man Annie was considering hiring at her market. Local shop owners arrived, too, finding their tables and spreading out merchandise samples. With each new arrival, Holly felt her tangled nerves unwinding.

By half past noon, the grove was buzzing. Some of the townspeople Holly knew by name, some she didn't, but almost all the faces were familiar. They were faces Holly had passed on the sidewalk or seen in Annie's Market. Now they were all in one place, breaking the silence with lively chatter—"Hullo!" and "How's your sister, Judy?" and "When does the music start?" Then there was Beatrice, her brittle voice somehow rising above the rest: "Don't crowd Henry! He's claustrophobic!" People lined up for scones at the buffet table and accepted the Save the Grove swag bags that Uncle Vincent was handing out. All the while, the day warmed and the mist lifted and the trees rustled to life.

Holly leaned against a tree on the edge of the clearing. She'd been afraid that nobody would turn out. Now she could hardly believe that they had. Her breath deepened. Her hair stirred in the wind. Slowly, it dawned on her: for the first time in decades, the festival was happening. Really, actually happening. And it looked just how she'd imagined it.

Well . . . almost. Where was Lionel?

She scanned the grove again, half expecting to spot him camouflaged among the arden trees in his Leaf Man mask, but no luck. There was another happy sight, though: Susan, Logan, and Pritha, weaving through the trees toward her. A young girl with jet-black braids ran ahead of them, squealing as she chased a squirrel.

"My daughter, Rosalie," Susan explained.

"She's the *cutest*," said Pritha. "Isn't she, Logan?"

"Hmm?" said Logan. "Oh—yes."

Susan snorted. "She's a terror."

"My uncle said you two sent a letter to the council last night," said Holly.

Susan nodded. "We're pushing for a halt to the factory's expansion plans until their waste disposal practices can be investigated."

"I think some of the councilmembers are here," said Holly, standing on her tiptoes to spot faces in the shifting crowd.

"Good," said Susan. She looked around for a few moments, then turned back to Holly. "This is great. Seriously. Nice work." Holly suspected that Susan didn't give out compliments often. She tried to take this one to heart, even though taking compliments to heart was hard.

Susan turned to Pritha and Logan. "You two get to work while I wrangle Rosalie." She stomped after her daughter, whose squirrel chase was about to create a buffet line collision.

"Work?" said Holly. "Are you taking more samples?"

"Actually," said Pritha, "we're expanding the focus of our summer research project." She nodded at Logan. "It was his idea."

Quietly and quickly, Logan said, "I was thinking we could add an element about how people connect to nature. How people come together to protect nature, like your committee, or celebrate it, like this festival. So it's not just about ecology, it's about—"

"Culture," said Pritha. "I'm interviewing my grandpa about forestry practices in India, and Logan— Well, you tell her, Logan."

Logan rubbed the back of his neck. "I thought I could maybe request to meet with Elders of a few different Native Nations for their insights."

Pritha pulled a notebook out of her backpack. "Is it cool if we ask people here some questions? How they feel about the grove and the festival, stuff like that."

"Sure," Holly said, surprised that they felt the need to ask her.

For a few minutes, she trailed Pritha and Logan and eavesdropped on their conversations with the townspeople. Many locals noted how long it had been since they'd visited the grove.

"It's funny, I was here so much as a kid. But life gets busy, and I moved north of town. . . ."

"I keep meaning to do my morning yoga here. I really need to make the time!"

"I used to walk my dog here before she passed away.

See that little hollow over there? That was Lulu's favorite spot."

Then, across the clearing, Holly saw him. Lionel. Her heart leapt . . .

. . . and promptly crashed. Behind Lionel was his entire family: Mr. and Ms. Madison, Ray, and Elise. Dread filled Holly's belly and silence rippled through the grove as heads swiveled toward the Madisons.

Lionel looked from his parents to Holly. He seemed frozen. Then he squared his shoulders and crossed the distance to her.

"What are *they* doing here?" she asked, trying—unsuccessfully—to keep the venom out of her voice. *They* were still Lionel's family. But *they* were also the ones who'd poisoned the grove and called Holly an outsider.

"Actually," said Lionel, "I asked them to come."

"You did? But *why*?"

Lionel glanced at his family. "The festival is supposed to remind everyone how cool the grove is. Maybe it'll remind my parents, too! I didn't expect them to come, though. It's weird, but I think they feel like they *should* be here, as . . . important people in town. Or whatever."

Holly watched as Lionel's parents looked around the grove uncertainly. His mom wore a dress, her usual sun hat, and heels—impractical for walking the grove, Holly thought. Beside her, Mr. Madison looked equally ready for a formal event in a button-up shirt with a collar so tight it appeared to be choking him.

"Are they going to cause trouble?" Holly asked, imagining just how it might go: the Madisons shutting down the festival, ordering everyone to go home, maybe even whipping out chainsaws and cutting down the trees right then and there.

"I don't think so," said Lionel. "When they're around a lot of people like this, they're kind of just . . . awkward."

When Lionel's parents returned Holly's stare, she steeled herself for a fight, but it seemed Lionel was right. Mr. Madison only smiled faintly while Ms. Madison pursed her lips. Lionel's siblings, meanwhile, were absorbed in their phones.

"Besides," said Lionel, "anyone who tried to ruin all this would *definitely* be the bad guy." He turned in a slow circle, taking in the whole scene—the lights, the tables, the people—then looked at Holly. "Magic."

"Hard work," Holly countered.

Then she remembered that she was still the festival manager. She didn't know what that involved, exactly, now that the festival was underway, but it had to involve *something*. So, while Lionel helped himself to the buffet table, Holly checked in on the Save the Grove Committee members.

Annie shooed Holly away with a smile—she already had several people helping her hand out food, including the man she'd just interviewed—and Reggie was done setting up his equipment. Miss Maisie told Holly that the table arrangement hadn't *quite* succeeded in preventing drama between local businessowners—Mr. Wilson from Wilson's Records 'n' More kept glancing at Uncle Vincent, and Mr. Butler from the cat massage parlor was "simmering in jealousy," according to Miss Maisie—but otherwise everything was going splendidly.

Holly grew exasperated. How was she supposed to be a manager if there wasn't anything left to manage? She marched over to Uncle Vincent. "What should I be doing? Nobody needs my help!"

Uncle Vincent scratched his beard. "Your next task might be enjoying yourself."

"Well, I don't know how to do that."

"Hmm. You could see if there are any new arrivals and welcome them to the festival." There was a trace of mischief in his voice. Holly's eyes narrowed.

Then she heard the twang of a banjo. Reggie's first set was starting.

While Uncle Vincent joined the crowd pushing closer to the music, Holly skirted the perimeter of the clearing, searching for new faces. Some people spoke to her as she passed by. They thanked her for putting together the festival. They told her she'd done a great job. And she was flattered but also annoyed because they were distracting her from her manager duties.

Then she spotted a new face. New to the festival, but not unfamiliar, and the last face in the world she expected to see.

"Dad?"

The man in the plaid shirt whipped around and flashed a megawatt smile. "Surprise! I've been looking all over for you."

"What are you *doing* here?"

He pulled her into a side hug. Holly was so confused that she forgot to hug him back. "Yesterday Vinny told me about the festival, and I thought, why not come check it out?"

"But what about your play? It's closing night! And what about Sylvia?"

"The guy who was cast as Lysander is feeling better, so I would've been back to Woodland Sprite Number Four tonight. And Sylvia . . . I haven't heard from her since she saw the play. Which is fine. You know, I was already thinking she and I are probably better off as friends."

Holly studied her dad's face. He sounded chipper, but sometimes there were little tells—a twitch in his eye or a split-second frown. "Well . . . I'm sorry about that."

He waved away her concern. "It was time for a new

adventure. So you put all this together, huh?"

"I had help," said Holly. "But I guess I did some of it. Or . . . a lot of it."

He gave her a funny look, like he didn't entirely recognize her. "Pretty cool, Holly."

She still felt confused. Was her dad there because he needed an escape from San Francisco or was he there for her? *Maybe both*, she thought, and she wasn't sure what to do with that. But seeing him there made her heart feel a little warm. She tried to hold on to the warmth.

"It's been a while since I've seen Vinny, too," her dad said. "Speaking of Vinny, where is that rascal?"

From the front of the crowd, Uncle Vincent looked over his shoulder and gave Holly a nervous smile. She didn't know whether she wanted to scold him or thank him or both.

"Vinny!" her dad hollered.

"Shh!" Holly hissed, grabbing her dad before he pushed his way through the crowd. "After the performance."

"Oops," he whispered. "My bad."

A familiar silence fell between them—the together-but-not-together silence, like they were trying to both land in the same dimension at the same time but weren't sure how. Holly felt overwhelmed by it all—the festival, the Madisons, her dad—so she tried to focus on Reggie's music. She'd seen his setlist and knew he was starting with bluegrass and jazz standards. With his loop pedals, he built each song from a single instrument to a full band sound.

"Who's playing?" her dad asked.

"Reggie Summers," Holly whispered.

"Huh. Never heard of him. He's good, though."

"We hang out sometimes," Holly said casually.

"This next song is one that I wrote for the grove," Reggie announced.

Holly had heard this song before, but she heard it differently now. She heard the way the percussion evoked a heartbeat. She heard the way the looped melodies twisted together into braids of sound that were bright and sad and mysterious all at once. *Places give you feelings,* Reggie had told her. *Sometimes I try to turn those feelings into sounds.* His song worked, Holly thought. It sounded the way the grove felt.

She watched the crowd watching Reggie. Everyone was riveted. Well, almost everyone. Mr. and Ms. Madison were whispering to each other, and Ray and Elise were still glued to their phones. There was something a little ghostly about the four of them, Holly thought, like in a certain light she might be able to see through them.

Not Lionel, though. He was up at the front with Uncle Vincent, dancing with a big grin on his face. He gave Holly a wave when he spotted her.

"Friend of yours?" her dad asked.

"Oh," said Holly. "Sort of, I guess. I mean . . . yeah."

Her dad gave her that look again, like she was a stranger he was meeting for the first time. The look made Holly feel embarrassed but proud, too.

When Reggie finished his set, he invited Holly up to the microphone, just like they'd planned.

"What're you doing?" her dad asked.

"I'm the festival manager," said Holly, lifting her chin. "I have business to attend to."

When she reached the microphone, Reggie helped her lower it on the stand. Her muscles tensed. She was walking a tightrope again, sweating in the spotlight.

"You've got this," Reggie whispered.

His vote of confidence steadied her. She leaned into the microphone. "Um, hi, everyone. Thanks for coming today. You probably already know this—lots of you have lived here for a long time and probably know way more about Arden than I do—but there used to be a festival like this every year in the grove. Like, a long time ago. And one of the things they used to do at those old festivals was . . . talk to the trees. Sort of."

A sea of blank faces stared back at her, but Lionel and the Save the Grove Committee members nodded encouragingly. She went on: "It's tradition. Everyone finds their own tree, and for a minute, you talk to the tree. Not with words, but . . . you let the tree listen to your heart." She looked at Uncle Vincent, remembering his words: *If the trees listen to us, it only seems fair that we listen to them, too.* "And you listen to your tree," she said, "because it's not fair otherwise."

Murmurs and giggles passed through the grove.

"I know it sounds weird. And I don't totally know how it works. But I thought we could try it. So . . . everyone find a tree, okay?"

Nobody moved. Holly's insides churned. She thought about yelling "NEVER MIND!" and disappearing and never trying to make anyone talk to trees again because it was foolish and frustrating and people were so difficult—

—but then Rosalie planted herself in front of a tiny arden tree and screamed, "MINE!"

That was all it took for the other kids to scramble to pick their own trees. The Save the Grove Committee members followed suit, then Susan, Logan, and Pritha. Finally, the rest of the festivalgoers began to wander the grove in search of unclaimed trees—all save a few, including Lionel's family, who remained in the clearing.

Holly found the tree with the crescent moon roots. Lionel picked a tree nearby. He gave her a thumbs-up, then faced his tree and pinched his eyes shut like he was concentrating harder than anyone had ever concentrated in the history of the universe.

Holly saw her dad, too. He'd also chosen a tree close to

hers. Still, he looked a little lost, like he was waiting for more instruction. Holly thought about helping him, then shook her head. He was an adult. He could figure out how to commune with a tree on his own.

Not that *she* was entirely sure how to commune with a tree. But seeing Logan, Pritha, and Susan at their own trees across the grove eased her fear of being unscientific, at least.

She took a breath and closed her eyes.

Hi, tree, she thought. *I'm still not sure how this works, but . . . you can listen to me, if you want. Like, my heart.*

The grove grew quiet—just the murmuring of the trees, and birdsong, and Holly's pulse.

And if there's anything you want to tell me, I'm listening, too. Well, I'm trying. Okay?

Holly wasn't sure what else to think, and she worried she was dominating the conversation. So she stopped trying to think anything particular at all. She just stood in front of the tree and inhaled the earthy scent of the grove.

Soon she felt herself sinking into the now-familiar ache. She tried not to fight it or run from it. And when she started to feel lonely, standing there in the quiet with her eyes closed and an ache in her chest, she reminded herself that she was still surrounded by an entire town. An entire community. If she followed the roots that spread out from her tree, and all the fungal connections that spread out from those roots, she'd run into her uncle, or Annie, or Pritha, or Beatrice, or any number of people she'd gotten to know over the past month.

Then there were the trees themselves. They were sick, Holly knew, but still standing tall all around her. Still casting shade. Still producing the oxygen that filled her lungs. Still communicating with each other, Holly imagined, sending chemical messages and nutrients through the roots and the fungi, figuring out how to survive. Figuring it out together. And now—more than ever—they had help.

The ache in Holly's chest didn't go away, but for the moment it felt a little lighter. She felt a little lighter, too.

Then conversation stirred across the grove. The tree-listening ceremony was naturally coming to a close—which was good, because Holly didn't know how to end it. As the mood shifted from quiet to festive again, Holly lingered by the tree with the crescent moon roots, unsure of whether she wanted to smile or cry or take a nap.

Holly's dad made his way over to her. "I feel like I should be wearing my woodland sprite costume for all this tree stuff!" He grinned the way he always did when he made a joke. "By the way, where is everyone getting those scones?"

While her dad checked out the buffet, Holly watched Ms. Madison waving Lionel over to her. Lionel and his parents spoke briefly and quietly. Holly gave them space but stayed close enough that she could swoop in to defend Lionel if needed—perhaps with a fallen branch as a sword and Henry the tortoise as a steed.

But soon it was over. Lionel rejoined Holly while Mr. and Ms. Madison gave the festival a final survey, their faces inscrutable. Then they turned to leave, along with Ray and Elise. When Elise walked-and-texted herself into a tree, Lionel giggled. "I shouldn't laugh," he said. "But every time I run into the sliding glass door, she totally laughs at me."

"Are you in trouble?" Holly asked.

"Not really. They aren't happy that I want to stay, but I put my foot down. Like, actually. I stomped my foot. It was fun. Anyway, they gave up pretty fast. I think they didn't want to cause a scene."

"But what about when you get home?"

Lionel shrugged. "The most they'll do is ignore me. And they already do that a lot."

Suddenly, of all the things the Madisons did that made Holly's blood boil, ignoring Lionel was the worst. But if Holly wasn't totally alone, she thought there was a chance Lionel wasn't, either. And he looked at her like he knew it.

"How'd the tree-listening thing go for you?" he asked.

"Okay, I think."

"I told my tree what I wanted for my birthday."

"I don't think that's the point—"

"My birthday isn't for another four months, so maybe it's too early. But four months isn't so long in the life of a tree, is it?"

"No," said Holly. "It's not."

"I can't tell you *exactly* what I wished for, because then it won't come true, but it had something to do with us being friends forever. Which means you'll probably have to come back to Arden a whole lot."

Holly scowled at Lionel. Why was he so ridiculous? Why was he so *nice*? "We'll see," she said. But when he smiled, she smiled, too.

Afternoon turned to evening. When the man in the bowler hat announced his scavenger hunt, Holly helped Rosalie decode the clues and nab the prize nestled in the tall grass: a snow globe that had golden glitter instead of snow. When Rosalie shook the globe, the glitter rained down over a tiny forest. Rosalie was entranced. Holly was, too.

Then Reggie kicked off his second set and the clearing became a dance floor. People swirled in the dusky light, their laughter infused with the champagne that Annie poured for the adults at the buffet.

When Holly and Lionel checked in on Annie, she gave them flutes of sparkling lemonade. She looked pensive. Lionel offered a penny for her thoughts. "I just wish my parents could be here to see this," she said. "But I'll tell them about it soon. And I'm glad *I'm* here to see this."

When Beatrice and Henry shuffled past, the old woman took one look at the buffet line and threw her frail arms in the air. "Nobody left any vegetables for Henry. The *nerve*!"

Holly looked at Lionel. "Is that what I'm going to be like when I'm old?"

"I hope so," said Lionel.

Then Holly spied her dad talking to Uncle Vincent. She got the antsy feeling that they were talking about her and made a beeline for them. When she reached them, they both fell quiet, which meant they'd *definitely* been talking about her. Holly planted her hands on her hips and stared at them.

"So," her dad said, "you like it here, huh?"

It took Holly a moment to find her voice. "Arden is small. And everyone here is kind of weird. But . . . I *do* like it here."

Her dad and her uncle exchanged a nod. "Well, maybe we could arrange for you to visit again soon. I wouldn't mind visiting more often myself. It's nice to, uh . . ." Her dad cleared his throat. "To check in on family."

Holly thought about giving her dad a casual answer. *Sure. I guess. If you want to.* Instead, she dug her heels into the dirt and said, "Yes. I'd like that."

She looked out at the clearing-turned-dance-floor. Susan was twirling Rosalie in circles while Pritha tried to get Logan to dance. He looked to Holly for help. She laughed. Then Reggie played a rollicking bluegrass song and her dad's eyes lit up. "What do you say? Should we hit the dance floor?"

"I don't dance," said Holly. "You know that."

Her dad pouted. "What about you, Vinny?"

Uncle Vincent's face was a portrait of sheer terror. "I'm with Holly. No dancing for me."

Her dad shrugged and shimmied his way into the middle of the clearing. Holly almost felt bad for him, but she knew he was fine. Her dad was always at home in a crowd. Soon he was outpacing everyone. Well, everyone except for Lionel, who was jumping and wiggling like his life depended on it.

Strange, Holly thought. She'd imagined the festival a lot of different ways but never as a dance party. Reggie seemed surprised, too, but he kept up the pace. His face was slick with sweat as he moved his fingers at warp speed across guitar and banjo frets. Holly hoped that when he was a world-famous blue jazz master, he'd still hang out with her sometimes.

"Not bad for two weeks of planning, is it?" said Uncle Vincent, looking around the grove.

"No," said Holly. "Not bad."

"I hope you feel proud of yourself, Holly."

She turned in a slow circle, taking in the lights and the

food and the dancing. The trees, too. Her shoulders relaxed and a pleasant sleepiness came over her. Then she looked at her uncle mischievously. "I heard Mr. Wilson was looking at you earlier," she said.

Uncle Vincent's cheeks reddened. "Oh? I didn't notice."

Holly giggled. Her uncle smiled and shook his head.

"Hey, Holly?"

"What?"

"I know your dad just said it, but I want to say it, too. You're welcome back anytime. Holidays, or summer vacations, or random weekends, or . . . Anytime."

Holly wanted to thank him, but words didn't seem like enough. So she wrapped her arms around him. He seemed surprised at first, but then he hugged her back, and the hug felt a little like home.

TWENTY-SEVEN

The plane pulled away from the gate. Holly's dad was so absorbed in recounting to Holly his starring turn as Lysander in *A Midsummer Night's Dream* that he didn't hear the flight attendant pointing out that his carry-on bag wasn't properly stowed for takeoff. Holly reached a leg over and kicked it under the seat in front of him. The maple syrup jars in his bag clacked together.

After Saturday's festival, they'd spent a couple more days in Arden. It had been long enough for her dad to fall in love with anything and everything maple-flavored, so he'd loaded up on local syrup at the Burlington airport gift shop. "I'll make pancakes at home!" he promised Holly, though she suspected she'd be the one who wound up making them.

When her dad finished his story—and before he could launch into another—Holly popped in earbuds. Not to listen to music, but just so everything was softly muffled. She didn't bother trying to get comfortable. Plane seats, she knew, were designed to be miserable. She didn't bother trying to sleep, either. She never slept on planes, despite flying often—and anyway, her heart was racing faster than usual this afternoon.

Early that morning, Uncle Vincent had woken Holly with news: Arden's town council had agreed to withhold the factory's construction permit until an investigation into the factory's waste disposal practices could be conducted. According to an article posted on the *Gazette*'s website, the decision was based on new revelations, including lab work conducted by Susan Morales and her students and a bundle of mysterious evidence delivered to the *Gazette* by a concerned citizen and her tortoise.

But when Susan had called to congratulate Holly, she'd said it was more than all that. "The festival showed the council that the grove still means something to Arden. If they want to be elected again, they'll think twice before destroying a space that just brought everyone together."

"But who's going to investigate the factory?" Holly had asked her. "And what if they side with the Madisons? What if the grove is still cut down?"

"One day at a time," Susan had said. "This is a win,

Holly. And wins should be celebrated."

So they'd celebrated. Uncle Vincent tried his hand at homemade waffles, and they only came out a little burnt. Lionel joined them for breakfast, and Holly insisted that her dad try some ginger-and-turmeric tea. Now, as the plane rolled across the tarmac, Holly's belly was full and warm.

She checked her phone. There was a text from her mom: Your dad told me about the festival. I want to hear more! Safe flight.

And several texts from Lionel: I already miss you. Do you know when you can come back? I want to start my next calendar countdown. Oh! Guess what? My parents think someone who works at the factory leaked the emails so I'm in the clear. But seriously, I miss you. It hurts. Ow.

She texted both of them back, then scrolled further through her messages. She didn't know what she was looking for until she found it—the text from Abigail, her sixth-grade science classmate. Hi, Holly! How's your summer going?

The text was a month old now. Much too old to respond to, Holly decided. But then, on a whim, she responded anyway. Hi, Abigail. My summer has been weird but good. How about you?

Holly switched her phone to Airplane Mode, wondering what might be waiting for her when she landed.

A few minutes later, the plane lifted into the air with a bone-rattling roar. She pressed her forehead to the small oval window and watched the world fall away. Just before the plane rose into the clouds, a tiny town came into view far below—a valley-nestled town of kaleidoscopic color with a bright emerald heart.

The cabin lights dimmed. Holly turned on her personal seat light and rummaged through her backpack. She pushed aside a bag of goodbye-for-now scones from Annie, a signed copy of Reggie's *Blue Jazz Expressions* CD, and the latest opinion piece from Beatrice, handwritten in shaky script (*Type it up and email it to the* Gazette *as soon as you get home. Don't dally!*). Finally, her hands closed around *Common Trees of the Eastern United States.*

On the inside back cover, she jotted down her Revised Fundamental Truths of Life. The first truth seemed fine as is, but the second and third truths needed tweaking.

1. Adults don't actually know that much more than kids (and sometimes they know less).
2. Olives are gross but sometimes they taste okay in pasta salad.
3. Lots of things don't last. But some places and some people will stay with you forever.

AUTHOR'S NOTE

The idea for Holly's story first came to me as I was hiking alone in nature one day. I was looking at the roots of trees along the trail and thinking about articles I'd recently read on the evolving science of trees—how they communicate in remarkably sophisticated ways; how they support and invest in each other. I was also reflecting on my efforts to connect and find community in a town I'd recently moved to. I began to ponder what it means to be rooted—to a town, to nature, to people, to ourselves.

While I already knew a bit about the wonders of trees, I had to do more research to write this book—and to gain even a fraction of Holly's tree expertise! There are two books in particular that inspired me. First, *Braiding Sweetgrass: Indigenous Wisdom, Scientific Knowledge, and the Teachings of Plants* by Robin Wall Kimmerer. In this beautiful essay collection, Kimmerer—a botanist and a member of the Citizen Potawatomi Nation—weaves together the knowledge of the modern scientific establishment with traditional Indigenous wisdom to explore our connection to the natural world. (There is a young adult edition adapted by Monique Gray Smith and illustrated by Nicole Neidhardt. Check it out!) The other book that had a big impact on me is *Finding the Mother Tree: Discovering the Wisdom of the Forest* by Suzanne Simard. Simard is one of the world's leading forest ecologists, and her discoveries about the connections between trees inspired many of the conversations that Holly has with Dr. Morales, Logan, and Pritha.

While the arden tree is a product of my imagination, everything Holly observes and learns about the trees in the grove—how their roots are linked by a fungal network; how they use this network to share nutrients; how the health of a single tree is tied to the health of the whole forest—is all grounded in the work of Simard, Kimmerer, and other groundbreaking scientists. And as Holly notes, the work of ecological science is ongoing. There's still so much to discover!

Like the arden tree, the town of Arden is fictional. However, it is true that Vermont—along with New Hampshire, Maine, parts of Massachusetts, and parts of southeastern

Canada—sits on the ancestral homeland of the Abenaki. You can learn more about Indigenous people from books created by tribal citizens. You can also visit native-land.ca and use an interactive map to begin learning about the history of Indigenous communities in the area where you live.

Finally, while it goes by different names, blue jazz—a fusion of bluegrass and jazz—is indeed a musical style! Jazz and bluegrass have distinct histories and create very different sounds through unique combinations of instruments, but the two genres have a lot in common. Both jazz and bluegrass players tend to be highly skilled and technical musicians who can play very quickly and improvise (come up with new music on the spot). You can find bluegrass and jazz fusion playlists online, but here are two songs to get you started: First, "Ramblin'" by Richard Greene, a bluegrass cover of a composition by jazz trumpeter Ornette Coleman (the original is great, too!); and second, "Spectacle" by Chick Corea and Béla Fleck, a collaboration between a jazz pianist (Corea) and a banjo master (Fleck).